Joan Taylor-Rowan

Katy Darby

Cassandra Passarelli

Sarah James

Helen Morris

Five by Five

Edited by

Cherry Potts

ARACHNE PRESS

First published in UK 2018 by Arachne Press Limited
100 Grierson Road, London SE23 1NX
www.arachnepress.com
© Arachne Press 2018
ISBN:
Print: 978-1-909208-61-2
ePub: 978-1-909208-59-9
Mobi: 978-1-909208-60-5

Printed on wood-free paper in the UK by TJ International,
Padstow.

Acknowledgements

Joan Taylor-Rowan:
Never Knowingly in Tales of the Decongested and Shelter's Stories for Homes 2018
The Bet Shortlisted for Asham prize, and in Tales of the Decongested

Sarah James:
Not Running shortlisted (under title *Winter Run*) in the first quarter of the 2017 Flash500 competition
Out of the Box in Flash: The International Short-Short Story Magazine

Katy Darby:
Tyburn Jig broadcast on BBC Radio 4, production company Sweet Talk 2013
Quarantine in Mslexia
The Nuisance in Slice magazine (US)

Cassandra Passarelli:
A version of *The Black Christ's Modest Miracle* in The Adirondack Review, Volume XII, no 1, 2011
Gorin in Salt River Review, volume 13, no 1, Spring, 2010
*The Pineapple Selle*r in The Sandhopper Lover, Cinnamon Press in 2009

Helen Morris:
LOL in the Bridport Prize 2015 anthology
Simon Le Bon will Save Us in The Goose Journal Annual review of Short Fiction of 2014-15

Editor's note

Five by Five is the first in what we hope will become a series of anthologies showcasing a handful of writers with a handful of stories (or poems). All the writers included here have been published by us before, often several times, and were invited to submit for this book.

The next in the pipeline is a poetry anthology which will be published in September 2018 *Vindication: Poems from Six Women*, which features writing from Sarah James (again!), Sarah Lawson, Elinor Brooks, Jill Sharp, Adrienne Silcock and Anne Macaulay.

Contents

Helen Morris

Joan Taylor-Rowan

DFL

Maya didn't want to leave Blackheath at all. She loved their little flat on the 'Blackheath borders'. She loved Blackheath village with its cafés and gift shops, and the church sitting on the heath like something from a Christmas card. She loved that it was called a village even though it was minutes from central London. Their flat wasn't in the best end of the street, but there were rumours that a Waitrose Local was coming. They already had an artisan bakery and a microbrewery. Just when they had actually managed to buy somewhere in a good area Robbie had this urge to move closer to his dad.

'Let's see the pictures then,' Maya's mum said. Maya dropped the estate agent's printout on the plastic tablecloth.

'I hear St Leonards is up and coming,' her mum added, in a too-bright voice. 'The arty younger brother to Hastings' old seadog.'

Maya rolled her eyes. 'Where did you read that?'

'I went online. It looks like the prices are on the rise down there. Gentrification, it's happening everywhere – even in Catford, although probably not on this estate. The rail link to London helps. Of course you'll be pricing the locals out.'

'I don't know what your mum's been reading,' her dad said, loosening his work-boots. 'I've heard it's still a shithole, drugs, alcohol, the lot. Have you looked at Broadstairs or Margate? I used to go to Margate as a kid, buckets and spades, jellied eels, candy floss. Loved it.'

'Hmm,' her mum said. 'There's a lot of talk about Margate, that's where that artist is from, the one who is always sharing her dirty linen in public.' She grimaced.

'You mean Tracey Emin.' Maya sighed, 'Professor of Drawing at the Royal Academy.'

Her mum hurrumphed. 'Well if you call that drawing.'

'I know, 'Maya said, 'your special needs kids draw better than that.'

'And don't charge as much,' her dad said.

She and Robbie had taken a look at Margate a few months back. Maya had read that it was becoming Shoreditch-on-Sea but with more edge. She'd seen three young pregnant women smoking in the shopping centre. If that was edge, then you could keep it. The creative quarter was an eighth and felt like a gated community. She could imagine the mob massing at the border, brandishing their pitchforks.

Robbie was a graphic designer so he could work anywhere as long as he could access London when he needed to, and he knew that she hated her job. The interns at the fine art auction house had sniffed out that despite her careful clothes and good grooming she wasn't one of them. She had a degree in Art History and some of them were barely literate but that didn't matter if your parents were titled. Entitled, that's what they were.

Her mum had been thrilled when she got the job. 'How marvellous,' she'd said, her eyes shining.

'I'm only a dogsbody,' Maya had laughed. 'I'm not writing fancy catalogues or anything – yet.' But now she was moving to St Leonards any hopes of scrabbling up the hierarchy were out the window. Her mum was trying to put a good spin on it, but Maya knew she was disappointed.

Robbie had loved St Leonards as soon as he got off the train. Maya had not been convinced. Down on the London Road, the charity shops were separated by empty storefronts pasted with leaflets and posters. Outside a newsagent and under the ATM that she'd wanted to use was a man lying asleep full-length on the pavement, his trousers wet around the crotch.

A teenage girl came alongside them.

'Excuse me,' she said in a wheedling voice. Maya turned.

'Could you spare a couple of pounds?'

Maya noticed with horror that she had no front teeth, just two incisors that made her look like a vampire. She recoiled shaking her head.

'Bloody hell,' Maya said as they took refuge from the rain in a greasy spoon. 'It's worse than Catford.'

'They're only people,' Robbie said.

'Barely,' she'd murmured and she'd caught that sideways thing he did with his eyes.

But they'd done it now – sold the Blackheath flat (it's in Lee, Robbie always insisted on correcting her), and bought in St Leonards, a short drive from Bexhill where his dad was now settled in a home for the demented.

'Don't call it that,' Robbie said. 'I know you're trying to be post-modern or ironic or something, but it's my dad and he's got dementia.'

She'd looked away, stung. It's not like he and his dad were super-buddies or anything. They'd only visited a handful of times before Robbie's mum died.

'He's all the family I've got now,' Robbie said. 'Soon he won't even know me and that'll be it.'

She could have said no and dug her heels in but she always felt it was Robbie's flat even though both their names were on the deeds. He'd put down the deposit and he paid most of the mortgage. Her job barely paid a living wage.

'No rush to find work,' Robbie said, when he saw her staring into the employment agency's window later that afternoon. 'We've made a bit on the flat. You don't have to jump at anything.' Chance would be a fine thing, she thought, scanning the window.

'Maybe you can chill for a while, stop trying to be liked by those rich freaks.'

She'd bristled at that. 'I do not try and be liked.' But she did, and the knowledge filled her with a burning self-loathing. Her brains had got her a place at Blackheath High and by year 10 her parents could finally afford to buy her the brands that she craved, but it had come too late. The invisible sign on her head called out to those who were born to see it – second class. She tried to talk to Robbie about it, but he was mystified. 'People like that are just a bunch of tossers. Why would you want to be around them if they make you feel bad?' She had no answer that she could put into words.

The house in St Leonards was big. They could have fitted their flat in it twice over. It had an enormous lounge and a spare room that Robbie said could be her studio when she took up painting again. French doors opened onto a garden.

'You can have parties out there in the summer,' Robbie said as they moved in their furniture.

She nodded. Saffron and Soo-nee might come but she would never invite anyone from work. She could imagine their patronising *wows* and *goshes* and *how charmings*, the way they'd shake their pretty heads back in the office and say how brave she'd been to make the move. It might as well have been Syria as far as they were concerned.

Their move coincided with a busy time for Robbie, so Maya spent her days unpacking and trying to put their old life into this new place. At the weekend they visited his dad. The nursing home was well maintained, with friendly but preoccupied staff. His dad sat in a sitting room with the TV on. It smelled of plug-in Fresh Air and school dinners. The staff spoke loudly and their peals of artificial laughter grated on Maya.

'Lovely to see you, son,' his dad said. 'When are we going home?

'This is your home for now dad, remember? We're only round the corner.'

'You'll have to bring that girlfriend of yours next time, the one who looks like Lena Horne.'

'She's here dad,' he pulled Maya forward.

'Is that you? You look different. Your hair's gone all short.'

Maya laughed. When she'd started at Barstow and Jolyon, she'd had her hair straightened, but she'd given up on perms and relaxers. She'd cut it short and let it grow naturally. She kept its dark halo in place with a vintage scarf – it had become her look. 'Very 'Bohemian',' her boss had said, running his finger around his tight white collar.

Robbie had taken out a deck of cards. 'Fancy a game, dad?' But his dad's eyes had begun to close.

They'd taken a walk to St Leonards Park in the afternoon.

'Well this is just like Blackheath,' Robbie said. 'Look at these houses. They're massive and only one doorbell each.'

Maya turned her nose up as she side-stepped some dog mess on the pavement.

At the top of the park Robbie stopped. 'Wow. Look at that view.' A verdigris sea nipped at an aluminium sky. He took her hand. 'You should paint this, Maya.'

Everyone knew what she should do, except her.

At the beach she turned to sit down. 'Eww! Gross,' she said. Numerous beer cans had been squashed into the slats between the benches which reeked of piss.

'Swanky buildings and then these scruffy, stinky benches; they could at least paint them. And why is there so much dog shit?' It was the thing her mother had obsessed about when she first came to England. 'Dog mess all over the place. And they had the nerve to call us dirty.'

'I think it's nice that old men like my dad can sit on a bench and have a drink and look out at the sea,' Robbie said. 'That's not a bad way to pass your days. Better than being stuck in a TV lounge watching *Homes Under the Hammer* at top volume. Just imagine if he didn't have us.'

Maya leaned over the railings and watched the seagulls picking up mussels and smashing them onto the pebbles below.

This is where they were living now. The future stretched out before her, bleak and unpredictable like the sea.

They walked home in silence. Robbie slipped into his study. The sound of Miles Davis oozed through the door and she knew he was back at work. She stood in the empty lounge, and stared at the high white walls. They needed furniture and rugs. They needed to turn it into a home. She sighed and returned to the kitchen to make lunch. In Blackheath her cupboards had been full of jars and bottles. The fridge had been stuffed with delicious things that she'd succumbed to in the seductively lit shops and the farmer's market.

She plonked a cheddar and Marmite sandwich in front of Robbie.

'The nearest Waitrose is in Horsham,' she said. 'I've just looked it up. And there's no farmer's market in St Leonards or even Hastings. Where am I supposed to buy decent cheese?'

'Perhaps you can have it flown in from France, or why not get your own cow,?' Robbie said as he typed away, shooting off emails.

She stared out of the window. 'Those chavs from the halfway house are dealing on that wall again.'

Robbie spun round in his chair. 'What is the matter with you!'

Maya jumped. Robbie never shouted.

'Were you always such a fucking snob...? Did I just fail to see it? If it's all so squalid and downmarket for you then go back and live in fucking Blackheath. Go and smarm around that creep Sebastian or Peregrine or whatever your stupid boss was called, if that's going to make you feel like somebody special, because I am beginning to think I don't know you at all.'

He slammed the lid on the laptop and stormed out and she heard the bedroom door bang shut.

Maya's heart was racing. She gripped the back of his chair. His anger seemed to hover like a solid presence in front of her. How dare he judge her like that! It was alright for him, he'd never been mocked because he didn't have the right kind of bread in his lunchbox or the right sweatpants for P.E. She grabbed her handbag and coat, tears spilling and ran out of the house.

She rummaged in her bag for her car keys. She just wanted to press her foot hard on the accelerator and take off. She didn't care where as long as it was away from here. Shit. She'd left the car keys upstairs. She glanced back at the front door. She'd just have to walk. She marched down the street her bag swinging, fighting with him in her head.

By the time she reached the main road, the rain was torrential. She stood under the bus shelter waiting for it to pass. After five minutes with no sign of let up, she flagged down the approaching bus. She'd go to the M&S in Hastings. Surely they would have Manchego… and pastrami. She'd buy up the fucking shop if she wanted to.

Maya hated getting the bus. Her eyes flitted around as she paid her fare. It was like that advert for the frozen veg, the ones who didn't make it to the Birds Eye factory – too old, too ugly too fat, too crooked. The bus was rank with the fug of stale clothes and cheap body spray. She brushed past a young mum at the front, foreign-looking, Filipina, maybe, and found a seat next to an old man and behind a woman with a shampoo and set.

'It's not very diverse down there,' Saffron had said. She was a journalist, one of Maya's successful friends.

'It's got a mosque,' Maya said.

'Yes, but it's very white, isn't it; full of racists who don't even know any black people. Those bastards are to blame for Brexit.'

Maya tried to think of any other black people she'd met at Saffron's famous soirées in her Islington flat, but she couldn't picture any.

The Filipina mum had a toddler on her knee, chubby and serious, his black hair like an acorn cap. He stared at the doors as they opened and closed. Someone cleared their throat, a guttural wet sound that made Maya want to retch.

At Warrior Square a woman got on with a little girl.

'Wait for me, Becca,' her mum called as the child began to search for a seat. Becca was wearing a Barbie puffa and fake Ugg boots. She swung on the pole as her mum picked up her shopping. The Filipino boy's steady gaze turned to the little girl. She grinned at him and waved. Her mother ushered her into the seat across the aisle.

'Now sit down there, Bex, and hold on. If you mess about, then no sweets for you.'

Maya stared out of the window at the sea; it had turned pewter grey. She wondered if she and Robbie would ever have kids. He'd thrown it in as bait to change her mind about the move.

'We wouldn't be working like dogs all the time, we could think about a family.'

She remembered how hard it had been for her parents to buy their flat, especially when her dad did his back in. Never enough money to make ends meet. Maybe that's why she had no siblings. They'd put all the effort into her and now she had failed them. She'd gone to the Boonies, the Sticks, the Provinces, the Back of Beyond, the Last Resort – there were so many names for the not-city, all of them derogatory. Robbie would make a good dad. He was so easygoing – usually. She felt herself flush at his remarks, and a wave of indignation rolled through her.

Maya watched as the Filipino toddler, transfixed by Becca, stretched his pudgy brown hand across the aisle. The little girl smiled at him and took it. Maya heard the Filipina mother giggle. Heads on the bus tilted indulgently.

Robbie and Maya had been in the first throes of love when his mum got breast cancer and Robbie felt bad that he hadn't visited her more often. They'd been really close when he was a teenager, he said. Her death had knocked him sideways. Maya had tried to get him to talk about his mum and his childhood but it made him irritable.

'I'm not giving you tales of the great unwashed to share with your Islington mates,' he said.

'I wouldn't do that.'

'That's what you say, but I've heard Saffron and Sunny.'

'Her name is Soo-nee, it means something in…' she couldn't remember. Blond, shiny Soo-nee had told her but she was too busy wondering if anyone's hair could be that colour naturally, to listen.

'It's Islingtonian for trust fund.' Robbie said.

She rolled her eyes. 'They're not like that, I'm not like that.' Maya sponsored a child in Malawi, or was it Mali.

Robbie's mum had died young and the funeral had been a bleak affair, bleaker than funerals generally were. Everyone was badly dressed, and the wake had taken place in a local community centre which had pictures by the nursery school on the wall and posters about diseases that you should watch for. The sandwiches on white bread had been sitting for a while and the smell of egg and fish paste filled the room. Who ate fish paste these days?

Saffron's mum on the other hand, had been buried in a wicker coffin and they'd sung wimmin's songs from her days at Greenham. There was a vegan buffet.

'So inspiring,' Maya had sniffed to Robbie as she blew her nose.

'Hmmm. She did look like she was going to heaven in a hamper though,' Robbie said, and Maya despite herself had gulped with laughter. That was the thing about Robbie; he could make her laugh like no one else.

The bus stopped again, and a feral-looking teenager with a mullet cut got on – *Eastern European* she thought. The Filipina mother untangled her child's hand from Becca's to let him through and as soon as he'd passed, the children held hands again across the aisle.

16

'Oh, look at that, just look at that,' the old man next to Maya said. For a moment she thought he might cry.

'I live opposite a nursery,' he said. 'They all play together, black and white, rich and poor – don't matter, just happily together. They can teach us something.'

Maya murmured in vague agreement.

The lady in front turned her lacquered helmet of curls, her eyes moist.

'It's like that film *South Pacific* where that white woman…'

'Mitzi Gaynor,' Maya found herself saying.

'Yes, that's her. She won't marry Rossano Brazzi because she finds out he has two native kids.'

Maya winced at the word.

'Shocking it was in those days. Live and let live, I say.' Her voice carried around the bus and several heads turned and nodded their agreement.

'Too much hatred in the world,' someone further up the bus said. Two or three people agreed.

'All you need is love…' the Eastern European boy suddenly sang.

'Na Na Na Na Na,' someone added. Several people laughed, and he laughed back. He was very good-looking, Maya noticed.

The bus stopped and Becca's mother began gathering her bags. Becca stood up. The little boy clutched her fingers. He began to cry. Maya remembered that moment at the hospital when Robbie had held his mother's withered hand. He'd known then, she realised, that this would be the last time he'd see her alive. She felt a surge of hot tears. Of course he wanted to be with his dad. The urgency of it swept through her like a tide.

Finally Becca's mum managed to pull her daughter away. The little boy leaned across his mother and pressed his face to the window watching as she disappeared. All heads were turned in the same direction. His mother cradled him as he wept, stroking his head and whispering soothing words in a foreign tongue.

Silence enveloped the bus. The grief, the love, the heartache, the hope, the disappointment, it was the same for everyone, wasn't it. Everything could change in a moment. All they had was each other, all they had was now and they had to make the best of it. A cloud shifted, the sun flashed and glittered. The sea turned to mercury. Something broke open inside her and she began to sob.

The old man patted her arm.

'You wouldn't do that if you knew me,' Maya wept. 'I've become such a horrible person and I never used to be. Everyone on this bus is nicer than me, and I've just had a big row with my boyfriend.' The tears slid down her cheeks.

'D.F.L., are you?' he said. She shrugged with incomprehension. 'Down From London.'

She nodded, wiping her face with the back of her hand.

'It's always a bit of a shock, but you'll find we're quite civilised down here. Here, have my hanky.' Maya shrank back slightly and shook her head. He cackled.

'It's ok. I don't really have a hanky... I use my sleeve.'

She laughed and then started crying again. 'That's just the kind of thing my boyfriend would say.'

The Dress

I know I must finish this dress. I abandoned it years ago, left it in the sideboard with the pattern still pinned in place. The tissue has yellowed but the cut fabric has no dusty crease marks. It's Shantung silk, with a square piece missing from one corner. I bought it on our honeymoon in Hong Kong. I didn't know what I was buying then, but its shimmer was irresistible. Michael paid for it – far too much – but it's lasted.

I have always sewn, always loved the feel of fabric, the smell of the starch, the bump, bump of it on the counter as the salesgirl pulls out the yardage.

Corinne phones just as I am working on the tailor tacks. They'll still be there when I pull the tissue pattern off – a delicate map of construction – like sutures holding a skin together.

'Hi mum, how're you doing?'

I say I'm fine of course; it's what she needs to hear.

'I'm making a dress,' I tell her. There is a pause and I feel irritated then desolate. Lately I've noticed her eyes flicker over the books I buy, measuring them, afraid that I might end before they do.

'It's just some old thing I cut out years ago, I'll probably never finish it but it's something to do.'

'Better than watching *Cash in the Attic,*' she says.

'Exactly,' I say laughing. 'I'll call it Cloth in the Cupboard.' She laughs too, a burst of sound, a release. She tells me about the children and I can hear them in the background, squealing and giggling and I want to hug them. She tells me she'll be around later, she has cooked me something. I place the phone back and notice how thin my hands are getting.

I begin by joining the bodice together, pinning the seams,

delighted that I can still estimate 5/8" with such accuracy. The dress has a seven-part bodice with princess seams and a shawl collar which comes together in a twisted knot. That piece, laid out flat, looks unpromising, a backward question mark – to begin a sentence with a doubtful ending perhaps.

I chose the design when I was slender with love. In the pattern books, full of lean models with arctic expressions, this one stood out. The girl in the illustration looked as newly married as I felt, her hands grabbing the skirt's fullness at either side as if she was preparing to leap. I got as far as the pinning, spreading the fabric out in the sparse living room of our first flat. It looked so perfect that I lay down and wrapped it all around me. In that moment, with the sun on my eyelids, I felt completely happy.

Three months later my waist had begun to vanish, an expansion that both fascinated and alarmed me. I stroked my growing belly wondering who on earth I was making. Corinne arrived, voracious and eager to grow. Eighteen months later, Cathy was born. Over the next seven years the unfinished dress, in its paper bag, disappeared under the holiday snaps, Christmas cards and Cathy's exuberant paintings – just an archaeological curiosity from another life.

The sewing machine is a treadle but it runs a treat. It was a wedding present from Michael's mother. It lasted longer than our marriage. It has always occupied the same corner of the room. Unlike Michael it didn't need more space. The machine sits on its purpose-built table – vintage they'd describe it now, like me I suppose, but I made all their clothes on this, sitting in the living room, laughing at the TV, listening for the sound of their hands clattering on the door-knocker.

I search around in the drawer looking for the bobbin and its case. I turn the hand wheel and the needle rises. I feel a little surge of pleasure as my feet rock back and forth, even though my hip aches and the pain in my stomach makes me giddy with nausea.

By the time I hear Corinne's key in the lock I have the entire bodice constructed.

It's astonishing sometimes to watch my daughter move around the room, fixing, plumping and adjusting pillows – to think that I created her – my DNA like a skein of thread, stitching the blue of her eyes and the red of her hair. I see Michael in her too, less evident, but there in her gestures, her robustness. At last she sits down and pushes the tea towards me, her eyes anxious.

'I'm feeling fine,' I tell her before she asks. 'Really. A lot better than last week, anyhow.'

She looks towards the sewing machine, and back at me, quizzically.

'You haven't used that in years... Why...?' Then her chin puckers, that little crease forms between her brows. She picks up a scrap of the fabric that has fallen on the floor. I know she has recognised the shiny threads.

I take a sip of my tea. Its heat burns my throat.

'I was thinking about the dress I made for your first day at school.'

Corinne nods, 'Do you mean the one with the apple blossom pattern on it, all green and pinks, like a painting?'

'Yes, that's it! I brought the fabric in Macready's when it was still a department store. I made one for you and one for Cathy. I have a picture somewhere of the two of you under the apple tree, wearing those dresses.'

We rarely talk about Cathy these days and I can see from the dip of her head, that she is wondering what it means, though she tries hard to hide her emotions.

'Cathy's was a different shape though,' she says quietly, twisting the thread of silk between her fingers. 'It was sleeveless because you ran out of material. So you put lace around the neck of hers, and I cried because I wanted lace on mine.' She clears her throat, gulps her coffee.

'Hmm, you're right. Fancy you remembering that!' I alter the photo in my mind, adjusting it to match her recollections.

'Gosh! All those things I made you; the fairy costumes, those shorts you both hated, the party frocks.' The clothes dance inside my head, lit by the vibrancy of my memories.

'You never taught me to use the machine,' Corinne says. She has forgotten that I tried once but she was too impatient. She gave it up for a game of hopscotch with the girls next door. I came back after lunch and found Cathy, aged seven, perched on the chair, her face screwed up in concentration as she joined two bits of fabric together with an erratic line. It was the beginning of a brief but intense love affair. When she cut out the square of my honeymoon silk to make an evening dress for her doll, I banned her from the machine and I made her hand back the material. I can't bear to think now about how angry I was. It was as if the last hope for my marriage had gone. She stared at me aghast as I cried and cried.

'Cathy was the one with the creative streak,' Corinne says suddenly. 'She took after you in everything.' She bites her lip realising what she has implied and looks stricken.

'I didn't mean… oh Mum, I'm sorry.' I wave my hand to show it doesn't matter. My darling Cathy – the wrong fabric perhaps, a faulty design, a built-in obsolescence that I could do nothing about. We didn't know about genetic disorders then but I feel guilty just the same.

'So what have you cooked for me?' I ask her, because even now we can't talk about the things that matter. I've begun saying that I love her, on the phone, and I can tell without seeing her face, that she's blushing. 'I know,' is the best I can get from her, the best she can do. Cathy would have been different and I am ashamed of that thought.

She opens her bag and pulls out a container of brightly coloured stew.

'Good Lord,' I say. 'It reminds me of a Mexican sunset.'

'Moroccan,' she says, pleased. 'It's a vegetable casserole. It's full of anti-oxidants.'

I grimace at the word. 'It sounds like something that will remove rust.'

'All the articles online say they really work,' she says.

'They say a lot of things,' I mutter.

'Maybe you should try another course of chemo,' she says, her eyes catching mine.

'I know exactly what my body needs,' I say. Her mouth droops and I wish I could snatch back those words. Everything I say now leaves an imprint. I try to scrutinise each phrase, judging its effect before I lay it out before her. I conjure up a smile.

'Does it taste good, that's what I want to know?'

She opens the lid and all my holidays return to me in one gush: turmeric and ginger, tomatoes and cumin. I close my eyes and remember the trip with Michael on the ferry to Kowloon, our clothes sticking to our bodies, the sun a white beach-ball in that impossible sky. I won't be able to eat it, but I keep smelling it, and listening to her voice. She hugs me goodbye and I can feel the healthy thickness of her flesh, its generosity.

I work on my dress into the night, gathering up the skirt. The last time I used this machine was the day she died. Trying to finish a dress she would never get to wear, pumping on the treadle like a marathon runner, cutting the last thread, putting a coin in the pocket for luck – a pocket made from that stolen piece of Shantung silk.

Michael was sitting in the other room when the phone rang, and when he came in, I already knew what he was going to tell me. I threw the dress away and never made another thing.

I think of Cathy on my chest, a dark pink bud scowling, naked and furious at her entry to this world. At least I will go from it well-dressed, she would have appreciated that. I have stitched both their names into the lining of the bodice.

I've spent too long up. My eyes ache and I feel a little sick but I only have the collar and the zip to do. I have decided to leave the hem unfinished. It is how I feel, I admit to myself. I have not reached my biblical quota and although I am an atheist I have always believed fiercely in that.

It has gone midnight when I pull it on, fumbling with impatience. I grab a scarf and wrap it round my waist. I twist until the light catches it. I feel tipsy with a sudden joy, like drinking moonshine. I keep having these moments of clarity, where I suddenly understand something that I've been struggling to grasp. I wish Corinne could share the beauty of the fire sometimes, instead of seeing only the destruction it leaves behind. But like a dream, the moment doesn't last. The light shifts and I see what she sees.

I drop into the armchair and the fabric rustles – its crispness almost painful on my skin. This is the last thing I'll ever make. For a moment the thought is unbearable. I want to scream and shout. I want Corinne to save me with her soups and good sense.

I clutch the dress for reassurance and let the morphine work its magic. I am in a scene from an old film. I am Cyd Charisse in chiffon, dancing towards a heaven painted in permanent shades of dawn. I feel infinity pulling at me and it would be so easy to give in. I smooth my hands down the folds of silk, and imagine Cathy laughing at me in my party dress.

'I've finished the damn thing at last!' I say to her.

Bitter-sweet, Like Pomegranates

(Inspired by Manet's painting, *The Execution of the Emperor Maximilian*)

It could have been my bullet that killed him. There were two firing squads and I was in the first; two shots each and the holes would be counted. I'm a soldier, I've shot people before, probably killed a handful but always in combat. I'm not like Ramón who feels his month isn't complete without some blood on his hands; we call him the wolf, which makes him proud.

I was a soldier before I was a father. I was late to fatherhood; I loved books more than girls my mother said. The friars taught me to read from the Bible, the words both sweet and bitter in my mouth, like pomegranates. Thou shalt not kill, yet I did.

I didn't volunteer, didn't want to be in the firing squad but not because I liked the man – what was there to like or dislike about him – he was an emperor, what did he know of my life? There had been rumblings in the streets. The hotheads spoke wildly of liberation – the French out – Mexico for the Mexicans. In the cafés the artists gesticulated, wild-eyed over their pastis, their girls in European dresses nibbling their pastries. We all knew that something was up, even though politics is only interesting when you are drunk and think that you have power, though the truth is you don't even have the power to hold your own piss.

The Emperor Maximilian was young. You imagine an emperor to be huge, strong as a bull but he was pale with a whiskered face, barely older than me. He was led to El Cerro de Campanas, his hands tied behind his back. He wore a sombrero and a white shirt stuffed with handkerchiefs to staunch the flow of blood. They said afterwards he wore the hat to show his solidarity with the Mexican people. Blond and blue-eyed, he stood in front of us with his two generals, Miramón and Mejia.

I heard he had done good things for the poor. Ramón said his uncle had received land of his own because of the emperor. It didn't stop him firing though.

I was thirty when my daughter was born. There are many children in Mexico, but they are not mine. I had only this one, a warm little animal with great dark eyes that looked at me and judged. When I held her in those first few days my hands felt soiled even though I had cleaned them with aloe against infection. She just seemed too good for me. I didn't tell anyone; men don't talk about these things.

The old people say toads can predict earthquakes, that when the earth moves deep below them, they stop singing and disappear; but there is nothing to warn you of upheaval in your own world, that sudden unexpected tearing apart that destroys everything. I lost her mother, three days later. She died in my arms, her hand resting on Consuela's downy head. The wind had picked up in the afternoon and a gust blew the curtain knocking a vase of wildflowers to the floor. I turned at the sound and when I twisted back, she was gone and Consuela began to whimper as if she knew.

A special reward had been offered to each of us if we would spare the emperor's face. He wanted his mother to see his body after his death. My cousin Diego stood next to me, the muscle jumping in his jaw. He had so many plans for the extra gold. From the corner of my eye I saw his fingers caressing the barrel of his gun. I thought of my daughter, how she likes to watch me take the barrel apart and polish it. One day she asked me where in the gun Death lived. I had no answer for her.

The Emperor Maximilian cleared his throat. His eyes scanned us and I wanted to look away.

'I forgive everyone and I want everyone to forgive me. Viva Mexico!' he said in good Spanish.

The priest arrived and covered his eyes with a blindfold. He muttered his prayers and anointed him with the oil of chrism. Maximilian gripped the hand of Mejia.

A crowd had gathered, leaning over the walls, some jeering and booing, others clapping him. I knew if I looked I would see faces I recognised. I had told the nursemaid to keep Consuela inside. I did not want her running into the square. I did not want her to hear the sound of the gunfire. I hadn't told her I would be there at the execution.

Love thy neighbour as thyself. Although I'd heard those words from the priests, in the Book, on the page, they were different – powerful and indisputable. Sometimes I think reading is a treasure I wish I had not found.

The sergeant ordered us to raise our rifles. The emperor shook his head as if baffled by the turn of events – how could it have come to this, he seemed to be thinking, what had he ever done but try his best? There was a distant shout and he turned his head in the direction of the palace, perhaps expecting even now, even as our seven guns faced him, that the Empress Carlota would come running through it in her embroidered slippers with some paper from France to save him.

In the street the *ambulantes* were plying their goods, chiles and *nopales*, papayas and mangos – things we feed to our pigs in a glut but unknown exotics in Paris they tell me. I wonder was he thinking of Paris as he stood there in the dust with the sun beating down. Was he thinking of European rain, his mother, all the things he would never get to see or taste again… the feel of his wife's skin?

'C'mon,' Diego muttered, 'I have things to do.'

'Christ, I need a drink,' Ramón whispered on my left. He lifted his hand from the barrel of his gun and cracked his knuckles. The sun caught the edge of the casing and it flashed. The emperor looked away, as if he had seen the light through his blindfold.

I felt the sweat trickle down my face, what were they waiting for? Mejia sobbed… at least I think I heard him. Afterwards I wondered if it had been me.

'Aim!' the sergeant roared and I saw a tremble on the emperor's lips. The scarf around his eyes was patched with sweat and my body was shaking too. The crowd was silent. The vendors' hands paused in their transactions.

'Fire!' and I closed my eyes and pulled the trigger. The sound was immense, my heart another blast resounding with the bullets. The air was full of smoke. I heard women wailing. We were ordered back whilst the next squad took our place. My heart was still galloping and I leaned on my gun to steady myself. The iron smell of blood hit me – the smell of the slaughterhouse. I refused to look. I didn't want to know if we had earned our 30 pieces of silver. I hoped I wouldn't fall to the ground in the heat. I heard a dog barking close to me and turned my head. Four men in red aprons came to take the bodies. I caught a glimpse of the white shirt – a red flag now. The church bells rang wildly. The sombrero floated on a pool of blood. I felt the bile rise. Ramón threw his rifle over his shoulder.

'Shit, man, he took a long time to die.'

'And his face!' Diego swore. 'That embalmer better sort him out. Half that money is already spoken for and I want to keep my balls.' Ramón slapped him on the back and laughed.

At home my daughter watched me while I tried to rest. I could see her through my lashes, her knowing eyes like her mother's. I have killed men before, watched their guts spill out over my hand as my bayonet ended them, war is war, but an execution – this was different. In my heart I think she knew that I had shaken hands with death.

'Let your papa sleep,' the nursemaid said, but I hushed her.

If the bar room politicians are to be believed, Napoleon had sacrificed the man, and Carlota, traipsing through the European courts in despair, had lost her mind. In my arms my daughter's flesh was warm and I thought of Carlota, wondering if deep in the cold walls of her European castle, mad with impotence and grief, she'd heard our bullets ring.

I did not know the man but his death seemed more honourable than my life. He did not have to see his daughter's eyes and wonder how he would tell a child who weeps at a fly's death that he shot a bound man at the behest of a foreign despot, a man guilty only of bad luck and poor judgement, of straddling the rift between two worlds.

And after death? Diego's prayer did not reach the ears of God. The embalmer let the body rot before he did his work. Those blue eyes that had seen the Palace of Versailles and the mighty Seine, liquefied. In the end they stole the brown glass eyes from a church Madonna for his corpse, and displayed it as a sort of triumph – but we got our gold.

It didn't change Diego's life. He avoided one villain but fell into the arms of another. By the end of the week, he was drunk and bitter and ready for a fight. It changed mine though. I traded in my serge with its reek of gunpowder and blood for a doctor's clothes, though I am no doctor yet. My daughter likes to see me with my books, traces the bones and muscles with her nail, probes for them under my skin with her curious fingers, feeling for the pulse of life.

Everywhere there are signs, beginnings and endings, endings and beginnings. I have confessed to a God I'm not sure I believe in. I have wept at the grave of my wife, and made promises that I hope I can keep. I have taken my gun apart and buried the pieces in the garden where the rust will eat away at them. Consuela plants her seeds there, watching with her serious eyes as they sprout and grow and bloom.

Never Knowingly

We decided to move into John Lewis in the second week of December. Spur of the moment, we said afterwards but I'd been thinking about it for months. We were sitting in the Collections department – a little bit like Argos but with manners and proper upholstery. Someone was thanking a member of staff for all the trouble they'd gone to, rather than all the trouble they'd caused. Roy just looked at me and I knew.

It's very busy in John Lewis in December and they take on a lot of temps. I know that because I worked there one Christmas, in bed linens – the best job of my life. There's nothing I don't know about tog values and interior baffles. One whiff of a feather pillow and I'm back there. Roy and I met in John Lewis – he did deliveries. He delivered me from loneliness I like to say and he rolls his eyes.

At first we packed a big suitcase and then Roy said 'Why? They've got everything we need – even a food hall!' and we laughed and laughed.

It was a Saturday early evening when we made the big move. We wandered about the store looking for the best place to hide until the shop shut. It was so busy. People seemed to burst in through the doors, their faces creased and angry, their fists clenched, then one spray later, smothered in Dior or Chanel, bathed in warmth and riding on a smooth escalator, their faces relaxed. Even the men didn't seem to mind smelling like Samsara. I knew we'd made the right decision but still I was nervous.

'What about the security cameras,' I whispered to Roy. He shook his head. 'Trust me they're all on the outside,' he said and tapped his nose.

Once the doors had closed and all the exits checked there

were no guards on patrol on the shop floor. Everyone thinks they have those motion-sensitive cameras like in Oceans 11 but they don't. We hid in the stairwell in a little recess that Roy knew about. He said some of the youngsters would go there for a snog in their breaks. Roy used to take one of my sandwiches in there – said he needed privacy for one of my cheese and pickle granary baps.

I could hear the sound of footsteps fading on the stone stairs, the muffled voices laughing and saying goodbye, and finally the silence, except for my heart which was going like the clappers. Roy had his delivery man outfit on, as a sort of disguise, although he doesn't do that anymore, in fact he doesn't have a job at all now which is the reason for the move.

It isn't nice to see your stuff on your front lawn, especially when you've spent all weekend mowing it. But what really upset me was seeing how shabby it all looked in the daylight, like a yard sale for the Brownies. Nothing looks shabby in John Lewis.

The first couple of nights were the worst. I found it hard to sleep. I'd forgotten about the cleaners, we had to hide until they'd finished with their hoovering. It tied me up in knots that waiting.

Roy was so calm. 'They won't hear us, industrial hoovers are noisy,' he said. 'As long as we stay in the shadows we'll be alright,' and he squeezed my hand. He's been like that since they put him on the pills – it's marvellous, like having your own personal rose garden that your head is always stuck in. I'm tempted to get some of it myself, but Roy says one of us has to have some perspective.

After they left, we spent two hours in the ladies' changing rooms until I felt my nerves calm down. We had such a hoot. You should have seen some of the things I tried on and Roy too. He's got a good pair of pins has Roy.

We soon began to forget we'd lived anywhere else. We dined on delicious salads and cakes – things I'd never dream of buying, always just about to go past the sell-by date of course.

'They'll only give this lot to the Sally Army for the homeless anyway,' Roy said. 'We're just cutting out the middle man.'

We were careful with our crumbs, just like it was our own home. We got up early, straightened our beds and I was very careful to put back the evening dress I'd worn the night before. I even got a little cleaning job to keep my eye on things. It was all just perfect, the Christmas lights, the big tree on the ground floor all covered in gifts and the smaller one in the children's department hung with little trains. Roy sighed when he saw it. We had to put his Hornbys on eBay, it nearly broke his heart.

And then I found the slippers. There were two pairs – his and hers, blue and pink bri-nylon from the Comfywear collection in nightwear. They'd been worn. They were tucked under the frill of a display armchair on the upholstery floor. They weren't mine and they weren't Roy's. I stared at those slippers for a long time.

That night Roy and I curled up on a swinging chair with our torch and I shared my suspicions. Someone else had entered our refuge. I blamed myself, we'd ignored upholstery and carpets – the heart of a well-kept home my mother would have said – and now we were paying the price. Roy wasn't convinced but he doesn't argue much these days.

At 11pm, wearing our black Damart all-in-ones and our faces dabbed with a bit of Cherry Blossom, we crept up to the top floor. Roy looked like one of those girls on the Clinique counter with his tan shoe polish cheeks and his black eyebrows. We crept up the back stairs and I listened outside the door.

'I can hear them moving around,' I said, peering in through the glass.

'Maybe it's mice.'

'With torches?' I scoffed. 'There is definitely someone in there, Roy.'

I could hear the disappointment in my voice. I looked into his face and saw my own emotions reflected there. I thought he might cry because I know I wanted to and then that feeling was overtaken by another. It surprised me really because I'm usually so placid, so accommodating, like one of those trees you see gripping onto the edge of a cliff in a high wind. Indomitable, that's what all the neighbours said when they saw my sofa loaded into the back of the DFS van and not a tear on my face. It was seeing that little tremble in Roy's chin did something to me.

I clenched my fists and I burst through the door shouting, 'What's going on?' in my best security guard voice. Their flashlights went crazy like two wild eyes rolling around in a monstrous head. Then the floor was plunged into darkness. Roy thrust the Maglite into my hand and I scanned it around the ghostly rolls of fabric and the swathes of curtains before bringing it back to the floor where it stopped. I heard a grunt surprisingly close to me and then a whispered voice saying, 'Hush George'. Four fingers poked out from behind a fixture, a cluster of rings on a wrinkled hand.

'Out!' I said.

She was short, permed, wearing a fleece and sensible shoes and huffing with indignation. George, her husband, was tall, stooped, about seventy I'd say, with tape on the side of his glasses, those awful slacks that old men wear, and shoes like a pair of battered tugs.

'You're not security,' she said and then burst into tears.

'Well you're not mice!' Roy said and he was right as usual.

I felt bad making her cry so I let George lead her to some nicely buttoned armchairs. I set the Maglite on its end and waited for her to calm down. She wiped her eyes and blew her nose loudly.

'So what are you doing here?' I said, still using my security voice even though I was no-one important anymore.

'We've been here since December 15th.'

'It was that advert,' George added, patting her shoulder. 'You see, we were relying on Doreen's pension for our home by the sea but she hardly got a thing.'

'It was crunched,' Doreen said. 'All those years in a job I hated. And then that advert came on with its lovely house and sweet little boy. I said to George, you know I think that John Lewis would understand – if we could just write to him.'

'Who?' I said.

'Mr Lewis,' George explained patiently, casting his hand around the dimly lit space.

'There isn't one,' I said. 'It's just a name – they're called Peter Jones in Sloane Square.'

'Well Jones, Lewis, what does it matter?' Doreen said. 'It's a man with money and we've got none and we wanted a Christmas like on the TV. I've earned it.' She began to snuffle again.

'Well you weren't careful enough. I spotted the slippers. You were lucky it wasn't someone else. We keep ours high up – top of the fixtures is good, or tucked inside a suitcase or a holdall. As long as you remember the combination lock it's a perfect hiding place.'

Doreen looked sideways at me. 'You too?'

'Since December 12th.' Then we all laughed, with relief I think.

'Our daughter is in Australia with our grandson. We were supposed to follow them but we couldn't afford it, but we couldn't bear the house without them,' George sighed.

'Roy and me lost our house.'

Doreen gasped, 'You poor dears!'

I felt sad for a moment just thinking about it, then Roy looked at his watch. 'It's Christmas,' he said.

'No Christmas presents this year, Roy. No tree of our own,' I said looking up into his American tan face.

'No house to put it in,' he answered.

'No family,' Doreen sobbed. We were all silent for a moment.

'Well why don't you come down to us,' I said suddenly.

Doreen stopped dabbing her eyes.

'Garden furniture – we've got a table that seats six and we're not far from the food hall.'

'Oh we couldn't eat the food,' Doreen said, appalled. 'That would be stealing.'

'You could stuff some money by the till – someone will think it got caught.'

'What a good idea,' Doreen said, and as she stood up I noticed the tag still hanging from her Gloria Vanderbilt jeans. 'We could go to Carvela and pick out some party shoes,' she said, her wet eyes all aglow, 'and there's a gold lamé dress I've been longing to try on.'

I gave her a look and she blushed. 'I'll wear a little top of my own underneath and we can put them back in the morning.'

I turned to Roy, his eyes had a glazed look in them and he was grinning like a pumpkin and I knew exactly what he was going to say.

'I'll go get that tree.'

We had the Rat Pack singing carols in the background and Roy and George rigged up some torches to give us the feel of candles – we didn't want to set off a smoke alarm. Doreen and I got Pictionary from the games department, the display box had already been damaged in the Christmas scuffle. You'd never guess looking at George what a laugh he is, I nearly choked on my oak-smoked ham.

When 'Ol' blue eyes' crooned 'Have yourself a merry little Christmas,' Roy put his hand out and I got up. I rested my head on his chest and tried not to think of the blue chiffon catching on the unvarnished garden trellis. We moved slowly around the barbecues and the garden chairs feeling warm and safe and happy. As the song came to an end, George stood up at the table.

'Here's to John Lewis,' he said, raising his glass of Harveys' Bristol Cream. 'Never knowingly under occupied.'

The Bet

I was eleven when Dana won the Eurovision Song Contest. I was rooting for Mary Hopkin because she was English but my mother, being from Derry, and my sister Bernie being a creep, were supporting the ninny from The North with the green hair-clip and the dimples.

We watched all those competitions, Eurovision, Miss World, Opportunity Knocks. It was a serious business in our house, sides were taken. To listen to us you'd think we knew Miss Argentina personally or had close connections with Greece and their satin-suited men with big moustaches. My mum always supported the land of her birth, my loyalty was to England because the rest of us were English and Bernie usually backed France because St Bernadette was French.

'But if Dana's from Northern Ireland like you,' I said to my mum, 'doesn't that mean she's British?' Mum gave me a withering look. My father sat on the fence. He was the Switzerland of our house but without the cuckoo clocks.

I had a lot riding on this particular Eurovision. I'd bet my sister Bernie a month's pocket money that Mary Hopkin would win. It was cash in the bank as far as I was concerned because our entries had great form; we'd had Lulu, and Sandie Shaw. After a whole day of considering, Bernie accepted my bet agreeing to pay me out of her savings account, an account better guarded than a chest of gold doubloons. She never spent anything on herself, preferring to take her pocket money down to the post office every Saturday and pay it in, poring over the columns in her book and scribbling numbers in the back, her pencil knocking against her teeth, her eyes up to the ceiling as she worked out some complicated interest calculation. Bernie was saving for her travels. She planned to move to Paris when she was eighteen, live near the Eiffel Tower and marry Sacha Distel. She tried to make me speak with her in French but I always refused, even though I longed to show off what I knew.

When she agreed to the bet I had a moment of uncertainty. If she was prepared to wager a month's pocket money, and not even on the French entry, could she know something that I didn't? Had she read stuff in the paper about Ireland's chances or was it simply the idea of taking money off me that motivated her to change her normal pattern? *Merde*! I'd been a fool to take on Banque de Bernadette, but it was too late now, I'd signed the betting slip.

Just to reassure myself, I wrote to my cousin Sean to get his view on it. We'd been writing regularly since the previous summer when we'd spent the holiday avoiding our families in a seaside town in Donegal. A year older than me, he lived in Derry like all the rest of my mother's family. He had a leather jacket and his own hi-fi and he knew what was what.

Dear Sean,

Thanks for your last letter. Hope it's stopped raining by now. etc etc ...

I paused and chewed my pen. I didn't have that much to write as my life consisted of school, hanging out in Woolworths, and trying to find ways to annoy Bernie, so I decided to get straight to it:

...It's the Eurovision next week and I think Mary Hopkin is going to win. Bernie's going for Ireland. Has the Irish singer got a chance? I'm getting nervous, I've bet Bernie a month's pocket money that the UK is going to get it. What do you think...?

The rest of the letter was filled with scenes from my uneventful life, my plans for the holidays and jokes from my joke book.

I think Dana's a dope, was his reassuring reply.

She's our entry. All the old grannies and the teachers like her. That should tell you everything you need to know. Is she really the best Ireland has to offer? I'm sure Mary'll get it...

Thank God for that, I thought, as I folded up the letter and put it back in the envelope, four weeks money was my entire savings, if Dana did win I'd be stony broke.

I sat eating my tea as the news rumbled on. Belfast was a city of burning cars and graffiti. The British Army stalked the streets dodging sticks and stones and running in their big boots. I glanced at the screen not really equating that Northern Ireland with the one of Sean, and my aunties and my granddad. Sean and his mates in Derry seemed to roam the place quite freely, picking up bullet cases and bits of debris, but apart from that he never mentioned it much in his letters.

He promised to send me a rubber bullet next time he wrote. I imagined it to be small and squidgy, a bouncy version of the metal ones. They were probably used like peashooters or tranquilliser darts, making the baddies jump and swear, giving them red welts on their arms and legs. Maybe I'd make a hole in it and hang it around my neck. I waited eagerly for my next letter.

When Dana won Eurovision 1970, beating Mary Hopkin into second place, I was outraged. Bernie jumped about the room, shrieking and clapping, and even though I called her 'une baguette stupide' it didn't dampen her glee. Mum was happy too, a triumphant smile stretching across her face. Bernie spent the rest of the evening with her savings book, and I avoided her, writing instead the words to Mary Hopkin's great entry in turquoise ink to post to Sean and wondering how I was going to survive for a whole month with not a penny to my name.

It was a week after the Dana disaster and I was doing my homework when the phone rang. I was pleased to answer it, anything to get out of Bernie's way. She was after me for her winnings.

'Can I speak with yer mammy, it's yer Auntie Mary here.' My mum took the phone and shooed me away as she closed the hall door. I groaned, that meant they'd be yakking for an hour and I wanted to call my friend, but then she reappeared five minutes later white-faced. Dad turned from his paper.

'Y'alright love?'

Mum was shaking a little. I felt a wave build in my stomach.

'It's my daddy, he's been hurt.' There was a croak in her voice. I tried not to breathe.

My father stood up, the paper slithering to the floor. Something had happened to granddad. Dad put his arm around my mother, a gesture that was so unfamiliar it made me feel uneasy. He sat her down, and she slumped on the settee.

'He was caught between the army and a mob.'

'Jesus Christ,' my father breathed.

I waited for her to tell him off, but for once she ignored his misuse of the Lord's name.

She pulled at her cheek with her thin white hands.

'Told the soldiers to stop, said he'd handle them, the fool,' She sniffed a little. 'They didn't see him or they didn't care, who knows, but they got him in the face with a rubber bullet.' My dad rubbed her back and squeezed her hand.

I breathed out and the wave retreated. He was alright then, it wasn't a real bullet. He'd be shocked for a bit, and would drop in to see the doctor for a check-up but then he'd be over to see us as he'd planned, with boxes of Lindt chocolate bunnies from his sweet shop and maybe some Milk Tray chocolates, the kind that came in a bar, with all the chocolate joining them together. I scampered up to my room, hoping that the drama would distract Bernie, but she followed me up, and stood at my open door.

'So that's £2.00 you still owe me,' she said.

'Honestly Bernie,' I said, 'how can you talk about money at a time like this?'

She dropped her head and poked at a hole in the woodwork with her finger.

'But you still owe it to me,' she said and slipped off into her own room.

I lay on my bed and thought about granddad. I'd spoken to him on the phone last Sunday. He'd told me he was coming over for a wee holiday. I thought of him outside his shop, trying to get a good look at the gang so he could have a word with them later. 'If you own a sweetshop, you know all the youngsters in the neighbourhood,' he used to tell me. I imagined the army man rolling his eyes as granddad called out. I pictured a little stout captain, with a twitching moustache and shiny shoes. I could see the dozy private letting the gun off and granddad suddenly slapping his hand to his cheek, darting around to see what yobbo had fired the thing at him. I smiled a little, poor gramps. He'd want to wait a week or so now while the marks went down but at least that meant I didn't have to give up my room straight away to his aftershave and starched collars and funny man smell.

I turned on my side and switched on the radio. It was Dana so I muttered *merde*, and turned it off again.

The next day my parcel arrived from Sean.

'It's from Ireland,' the postman said, rattling it. 'I hope there's not a bomb in it.'

I stared at him then closed the door without saying thank you. Up in my room I undid the packaging. It was heavy and I guessed Sean had sent me something else too. I tore off the paper and unfolded the tissue. There was a big black solid object inside, almost as big as a toilet roll tube with a pointed end. I poked it. It was hard like a car tyre. This must be some other bit of hardware he'd found. I rummaged through the paper for my little bullet but there was nothing else there. I opened the note.

Thanks for the song lyrics. She really should have won. Here's a rubber bullet like I promised, shame about Dana, and your bet. Hope you didn't lose too much.

love Sean

I dropped the bullet on the bed, afraid to touch it. I wanted to be sick. My granddad had been hit in the face with one of these?

I stared at it for a minute then picked it up again gingerly with a bit of tissue, and buried it in the bottom of the drawer under my jumpers. I went into the bathroom, locked the door and filled the bath. I sank into its burning depths until my skin turned pink and even my head was covered. Under the water everything was blurred and booming. My eyes smarted in the soapy water. I rubbed them trying to stop myself from imagining his damaged face. I stayed there until the water went cold and my fingers were as wrinkly as granddad's.

I went to school the next day but I didn't tell anyone what had happened. I thought about the bullet in the drawer, and wondered what I should do with it. Poor Sean would be feeling terrible that he'd sent one to me. When I got home it was my father who let me in. I stared at him and he looked away. I hesitated for a moment, afraid to let go of the door jamb. Bernie was already there sitting on the sofa, still in her blazer. I went upstairs to my room and took off my coat. I tried not to look over at my chest of drawers, but I couldn't help it. I had the feeling that if I opened it, the thing would burst out huge and dark like a Zeppelin, swallowing up the room and suffocating me. I took £2.00 out of my money box and hurried downstairs.

'Will you sit down please Claire,' my dad said in a strangled voice. 'I have some very sad news for you.'

I dropped onto the settee, and held Bernie's hand, pressing the money into it at the same time.

'It's okay,' she whispered, her voice shaky. 'You keep it. Mary should have won.'

My eyes welled up and the tears began to roll down my face. I squeezed the dry notes and her damp fingers, and she squeezed mine back.

'Merci' I said. 'Merci beaucoup.'

Katy Darby

Cuckoo

Night. Quiet. A haze of moonlight seeping through the thin curtains like blood through gauze. The breathless, foetid-fresh smell of a child's bedroom.

Mummy stands, her hand still on the doorknob, touching it lightly, like a chess player lingering over an uncertain move. She can hear her own hushing breath as her eyes adapt to the soupy darkness. She can't hear his, though, which means that he is awake and pretending to be asleep for her benefit. She wonders when he will learn deception, how to mimic the pale snores and gasping snuffles of true sleep. She learned early on, aged six or seven, and remembers thinking that she was a very clever little girl. She still pulls that trick sometimes, when Daddy comes home late and she doesn't want to speak to him. She does a very good imitation of a peaceful sleeper, which is ironic, as her own slumber is often violent and disturbed. She still suffers from the nightmares of her childhood.

'Nicky?'

He doesn't respond. She pictures his large blue eyes upturned to the invisible mobile dangling from the ceiling. Ships and balloons and trains and planes and cars. He loves machines, motors, anything that can get you from place to place; he's not fussy. She moves further into his room, letting go of the doorknob but not closing the door behind her. The landing, too, is dark, but already she can see more, make more sense of the grainy, pullulating shadows. She tiptoes forward and kneels softly on the thick carpet, her head near his. Only the crack of tendons in her knees gives her away. She senses him flinch at the snap, or her nearness, she doesn't know which. She lays her hand on his forehead and strokes back his soft, fine hair. Warm and clammy, but better than a few hours ago. Less feverish. He is still pretending to be asleep.

'Nicky,' she whispers, 'are you feeling better now?'

He does not move, does not answer, a hot, angry little corpse.

'I'm sorry you couldn't go to the fair, sweetie,' she says. 'You had an awful temperature. We couldn't let you, really.'

Silence. He's sucking in stiff shallow breaths, lying motionless, rigid with righteousness. She thinks she can make out the rise and fall of his ribs, and is reminded of dogs panting, or mice; the smaller an animal, the faster it breathes. If you could listen to a mouse's heartbeat it would blur into a constant high thrum.

'Mummy and Daddy couldn't go either,' she says.

Instead they had enjoyed a rare, relaxed dinner at home over a bottle of wine, both keeping an ear out for the baby monitor. Nicky had wept and grizzled and yelled as far as his sore throat allowed, and even though they had said he could watch the big fireworks on the TV in his room as a special treat – and the big fireworks were bound to be better than the modest local bonfire night, Daddy had assured him – he had refused. It wasn't the same. He wanted to be there.

Mummy remembers how much Nicky had loved November 5th last year: the smell of wood-smoke on leather jackets, the creamy, salty taste of fire-blackened chestnuts, the crowds coddled in scarves and warm coats, flush-faced beneath the sudden light of exploding stars. How everybody had looked younger, guiltless, in the glow of flames and fireworks. And the games, the fairground stalls; the hot, slapdash smell of carnival food, the lights in the darkness, people shouting to one another over the barkers and fluorescent music, breath billowing like dragonsmoke.

'Silly Nicky,' she says, 'don't sulk now. You can go next year.'

How can she have forgotten the yawning scale of childhood time and space, when a year might as well be a million, where the bottom of the garden is the end of the world? She hasn't forgotten that Nicky hates being called silly.

'I'm not silly,' he says fiercely, forcedly, reluctant to break his silence but stung into defending himself. She smiles at his profile in the darkness.

'Of course not, sweetie. Sorry. Just ill and a bit tired.'

A grumpy pause.

'I wasn't even that ill. I could have gone.'

Time to be strict, she knows. She hardens and deepens her voice. How much of parenthood is play-acting, storytelling.

'Yes, Nicky, you were. You were burning up.'

'Like a bonfire,' he says, sulkily.

'Exactly like a bonfire,' she says, brisk and businesslike. She modulates her tone again. 'A cross little bonfire. But I'm glad you're feeling better now.'

'A bit,' he admits, a grudge in his voice. She reaches out to where she knows the bedside table to be and places the beaker on it gently.

'There's some water,' she says, 'and if you want anything in the night we're just across the landing. You go to sleep now.'

She leans over to kiss him on the forehead but he stops her.

'No,' he says.

A weird cold washes through her.

'No what, Nicky?'

'I can't go to sleep without a bedtime story. I want a story.'

His tone is plaintive, and she realises that of course, because he had been dozing on and off with the temperature and the fever, they have not followed the usual night-time ritual. He hasn't been put to bed properly; of course he can't sleep. His night-light, a rubber bulb that glows a soft angry orange when pushed into a plug socket, has not even been switched on.

'I'll have to turn the lamp on, then.'

He twists away from her as though from a fire.

'No, it hurts my eyes.'

'Well, darling, I can't read you a story in the dark. Mummy needs light to see.'

'Can't I have a new story?'

'What sort of story?' she asks, playing for time, wondering whether she isn't too tired to make up a satisfying tale at this time of night. Calling Daddy won't be much help; Nicky complains that his stories are boring.

'A story about Bonfire Night.'

'Guy Fawkes?'

He shakes his head; she sees the movement and hears his hair flap vigorously on the pillow.

'Boring. We did it at school.'

He's only been going to school for a year or so, but he is already world-weary, blasé about painting and reading and break.

'Oh. Well then.'

'A new story,' he insists. She sits back on her heels, then eases the cramp in her calves by manoeuvring into a cross-legged sitting position on the carpet by the bed. Her mouth is exactly on a level with Nicky's ear.

'All right then,' she says, not at all sure of what she is going to say next. She feels a brief flash of the vertiginous terror actors must experience when they dry on stage.

'What's it about?' he demands.

'Bonfire Night.'

He wriggles impatiently. 'And?'

'A little boy.'

'A little boy like me?'

'A little boy very much like you. He had big blue eyes, and messy blond hair, and he had a Mummy who was very much like me.'

'Oh good,' Nicky says, approvingly. Her confidence is buoyed like a balloon on an updraught. Write what you know, isn't that what they say?

'Once upon a time – on a night very much like tonight, in fact, a November 5th not very long ago at all, the Mummy of this little boy decided to take him to see the fireworks on the village green.'

'Was he ill?'

'No,' she says firmly. 'He was a very healthy little boy and had absolutely no temperature at all, which was why she decided to take him.'

'Did his Daddy come too?'

'No, darling, the little boy's Daddy was away at work that weekend, in France. But he wished he had been there, and so did his Mummy, especially after what happened that night.'

She hears him stir, tense, curl himself up into a tight little ball of delighted anticipation. Now she's got him.

'What happened?'

'We'll see. I'll tell you about the bonfire night first.'

'All right.' A fire, almost as good as a mystery; not quite.

'There was a huge bonfire. Blazing.'

'How huge?'

'Very. Bigger than Daddy.'

'Bigger than a house?'

Mummy considers.

'No, not quite as big as a house. Maybe as big as the garden shed. But very big and very hot, with flaming sparks shooting out of it, and wood glowing red-hot so you couldn't go too close to it without your hair crisping up and your face going bright red.'

'Really hot?'

'So hot you couldn't toast marshmallows.'

'Why not?'

'Because they wouldn't melt, they'd just explode in pink smoke.'

'Cool.'

'And the fireworks were the best fireworks you've ever seen. They'd been brought all the way from China where people had made fireworks for thousands of years.'

'Thousands...' Nicky says softly, impressed.

'They were in the shapes of stars and moons and wheels and planets –'

'Were there rockets?'

'Yes, and when they exploded they filled up the sky with sparkling rain in gold and silver and blue and green and pink.'

'Rainbow rain,' says Nicky.

'Yes, rainbow rain. Like glitter. And the bang was so loud that the church wobbled.'

Nicky giggles.

'But before anyone could watch the firework display, first of all the little boy and his Mummy went to the fairground and had a go on all the games.'

'All of them?'

'Every single one.'

'What was there?'

She tries to remember from last year. All that springs to mind are the gentler, less exciting attractions, the stuff of Victorian nostalgia; the hook-a-duck stall, the hoopla and tombola, the lucky dip. She thinks of other fairgrounds, all the festivals and carnivals of her life.

'There was a … ghost train. And a rollercoaster, just for one night, that looped around the bell tower twice and finished on the cricket pitch. And there were stalls selling toffee apples and popcorn and candy floss, blue and pink and yellow candy floss, and hot dogs and hot chocolate and chestnuts and it all smelled delicious and amazing. And there was a shooting gallery, too, where you had to get three shots right in the middle of the target to win a goldfish, or a toy lion, or a cowboy hat, or – '

'What else?'

Mummy is running out of inspiration.

'There was a hall of mirrors, and a darts game, and hoopla.'

'What's hoopla?'

'It's where you have to throw a wooden ring over a pole to win a prize.'

'What prize?'

'Well, there were all sorts of stuffed toys, great big ones, nearly as big as the little boy himself. Every animal you could imagine. Kangaroos and elephants and giraffes. Whales and dolphins and dinosaurs.'

'Bears too?'

'Of course.'

'Bears like Big Bear?'

Mummy involuntarily glances to where Big Bear sits, a fuzzy patch of blacker darkness in the shadowed corner. He is propped up in Nicky's half-size blue rocking chair, unmoving and silent, his weighted forepaws resting on the arms of the chair like the clenched fingers of a hanging judge.

'Just like him,' she says. 'All hanging from the ceiling where nobody but the stall holder could reach.'

'Did Mummy play the hoopla?'

'Oh yes,' she says vaguely, 'eventually.'

'What did she win?'

'Ah,' says Mummy, cryptically. 'That's a very good question.'

Nicky scrunches himself up with excitement.

'Why?'

She takes a deep breath and wonders.

'Because when the little boy and his Mummy were going through the fair, the little boy saw the blue candy floss and wanted some. He'd never seen blue candy floss before.'

Nicky scoffs. He'd seen it last year, ages and ages ago. He'd eaten so much of it that he'd been sick in the car on the way home. The sick hadn't been as blue as he'd hoped.

'So, anyway, the little boy was quite a bit littler than you and he was in a pushchair to that his legs didn't get tired.'

Again Nicky, normally robust to a fault, looks smug in the near-dark.

'And while his Mummy was talking to the stall holder and waiting for the blue candy floss to give to her little boy, guess what happened?'

Nicky cannot imagine.

'When she looked down at the pushchair again, her little boy was gone!'

Nicky gasps with excitement.

'Run away?'

'No,' Mummy says firmly, 'although she did think that for just a second, because he'd vanished like a puff of smoke. But what made her realise that the little boy hadn't run away, that he'd actually been kidnapped, was what was in the seat of the pushchair instead of him. What do you think it was?'

Nicky shakes his head dumbly.

'Go on, have a guess.'

'A ghost?'

'No.'

'A little girl?'

'No.'

'A candy floss?'

'Now you're being silly. Shall I tell you?'

'Yes.'

'It was a large stuffed bear, almost exactly the same size as the little boy she had lost. He had soft brown fur like Big Bear, and shiny black eyes like Big Bear, and big heavy paws too. In fact –' she cocked her head at Big Bear, silent in the chair, still and dumb, '– he was very, very much like Big Bear in every way.'

'What did she do?'

'Well, first of all she screamed. She screamed very loud, so that everyone turned around and even the carousel stopped in surprise. And then she started pushing the chair with the bear in it all around the funfair, running over people's toes and bumping into them, spilling their drinks and their hot dogs and crying and shouting that somebody had stolen her son.'

Nicky's eyes are wide and luminous, glowing pale grey at her in the iron-coloured shimmer of the room.

'What did they do?'

'Do? They got out of her way. They thought she was mad, poor woman, running through a fairground screaming and weeping with a stuffed bear in a pushchair. But she wasn't mad. Someone really had stolen her son and put a soft toy in his place.'

'Why?'

'It's called a changeling.'

'What's a changing?'

'Do you remember the story of the Ugly Duckling?'

Nicky looks uncertain.

'Yes…'

'Like that. Except that because all eggs look the same, the ducks didn't know he was a swan until too late.'

Nicky absorbs this. He is beginning to relax a little again: the Ugly Duckling, after all, has a happy ending, like all good stories.

'What happened then?'

'Well, she started going up to all the stallholders, to ask if they had seen anything, if they'd seen somebody carrying her little boy. She described him in every detail but nobody had seen anything. And just when she had almost given up, she came to the last stall.'

'Which stall was it?'

'It was the hoopla. The throwing-rings game, remember?'

Nicky blinks and nods. His face, which this morning had been flushed with fever, is milky pale. He lays his head back gently on the pillow, not moving his eyes from hers for a second.

'And guess what she saw dangling from the ceiling of the stall, hung up on a hook by the straps of his dungarees, looking very confused but perfectly all right?'

Nicky smiles.

'Her little boy!'

Mummy strokes his warm soft cheek.

'Clever you. That's right. So what do you think she had to do?'

'She had to win him back?'

'Exactly. She couldn't get past the stall holder to rescue him, because the stall holder was big and strong – bigger than Daddy

– and he wouldn't let her. He said he had no children, and that he needed a son to help him on the stall, and that if she couldn't win her little boy back fair and square, he would raise the child as his own and all she would have to take home was a stuffed bear. So he gave her three hoops and told her she had to get all three over the pole to win her boy back. Normally you only have to get one ring over to win a prize.'

'All three?' Nicky's eyes are wide with indignation.

'Yes, because the little boy was the top prize, the most precious thing, and so she had to be extra good to win him back.

'So she narrowed her eyes, took a step forward and squinted at the pole, measuring the distance. She took the first ring in her hand – and even though her hands were shaking and her heart was shivering, she threw it straight and true and it rattled down over the pole easily. The same thing happened with the second ring. But just as she was throwing the third ring, she felt something soft touch her leg, and she jumped and screamed. She had forgotten all about the bear, and it had fallen out of the pushchair against her leg. Or at least that's what she thought at the time. When she jumped she let go of the ring and it bounced and banged around the pole – it almost looked as if it might still just go over, but then it bounced one last time and fell down on the ground.

'She had lost, and the stall holder laughed a terrible laugh and told her to keep the bear, that it could be her booby prize. She tried to climb over, to rescue her son, still dangling from the ceiling by his dungarees, but the stall holder pushed her away and none of the onlookers would help her. She stumbled away, sobbing, with nothing but the pushchair and the bear.'

'How did she get him back?' asked Nicky curiously. For she must have got him back? He was here, wasn't he, with her now?

Mummy's eyes are glazed a little with tiredness. In the twilight of Nicky's bedroom she looks far away, like someone in a mirror.

'She didn't, Nicky,' she says quietly, gently. 'She had to take another little boy out of his pushchair while his Mummy was buying a toffee apple. She put Big Bear in the little boy's place and hoped that the other Mummy wouldn't notice. And she didn't. Not until it was too late anyway.'

She glances across at Big Bear's corner. 'Big Bear came back, of course. Followed them home. He needed a Mummy too.'

Nicky blinks. Mummy glances at her watch, its face, like hers, unreadable in the darkness. Then she suddenly smiles wide. He can see her teeth and eyes gleam.

'Well, it's time to go to sleep now, Nicky. Good night and God bless.' Mummy stands up, knees crackling like firewood, and leans over to kiss Nicky on his dry cheek. As she moves towards the door, she flicks on the night light. Two sparks of orange flame ignite in the rocking-chair corner, where Big Bear's shiny black eyes outstare the night. Mummy yawns and pauses as she opens the door of Nicky's bedroom.

'Silly Mummy,' she whispers tenderly, 'I forgot the most important part. They all lived happily ever after.'

The Tyburn Jig

She'd promised herself two things, today: that she'd not lose sight of him, and she'd not cry. The first should've been easier, by far; but now, pushing through the raucous execution-day crowd full of people seeming to possess considerably more elbows and knees than they had any right to, she wasn't so sure.

Sarah Middleton was a small woman, not above five feet three inches high, even in her heeled and buckled shoes. A big man like Fred might span her tiny waist with two hands, and a few had tried before Fred saw them off.

She was dressed entirely in black, today; not in anticipation of her imminent widowhood, but because that's what Mrs. Grainge insisted her employees at the milliner's wore, even those stuck in the workroom behind the shop, who never saw the customers. Sarah would have to work late tonight: she only had a half-day off, and that given grudgingly, for she'd told nobody that her husband was to hang today.

Sarah had invented an ailing relative, but in the noonday heat and crush she couldn't now recall whether it was a great-aunt or a second cousin. *What tangled webs we weave,* she thought, trying to shake the ache from her head. Mrs. Grainge was sure to remember, and sure to ask, in that casually polite way that meant she suspected you in a lie. Sarah wished she'd made a note somewhere; wished she carried a pocketbook like Fred always did, though it was that put the noose about his neck, in the end.

It was good weather for a hanging, though not for Sarah: the road would stay dry and dusty all the way to the Triple Tree, and the hawkers would rake in the pennies from ballad-sheets and pies. Fred wasn't the only condemned man being dispatched today, of course: sharing the cart were a horse-stealer, a highwayman and two prolific pickpockets, whose pals would probably be working the crowd even as a brace of their own danced the Tyburn Jig.

The mourning bells of St Sepulchre tolled slow and sonorous and those nearest the gaol's black gate muttered in anticipation. A creak, a squeak, a neigh: the crowd belly-roared and they came out, and not before time – the noon-bell's last echo was already dying away. Three of the fellows were badly dressed, shabby as London sparrows, but there was one who was almost a Macaroni, with a tall white wig and a pea-green coat, and another who'd donned his wedding-suit to kiss the hangman's daughter.

Sarah had heard a few of the condemned did that. She supposed it was a joke; she thought it in awful poor taste. She willed the fellow in green to turn round: it must be Fred, he always was a dandy and he loved his coloured silks. His hands were bound behind him, already bloodless and white: her heart throbbed for him, stupidly, and she scolded it.

Someone in the crowd shouted 'Stand and deliver!' There was a burst of laughter and the green-jacketed man turned around, revealing a pocked complexion and a hooked nose. Robert Dare, the highwayman, then; not Fred, not Fred at all! Sarah's hand flew to her mouth. She should not care. She would not cry. Not even though Fred was wearing the suit she'd last seen on their marriage-day for a second, hempen wedding. He'd been so handsome that day! She should never have wed him. Even then, she'd known.

The City Marshal and his men rode out, surrounding the execution-cart; some of the mob turned from pelting the pickpockets with corn-husks and rotten potatoes to try their aim at the uniformed guards, bright and upright in the glaring sun. One guard fired his rifle in the air and yelled: cowed, the rabble fell back and the slow procession began. The two miles to

Tyburn would take as many hours with such a press of people on the streets. Two hours to live, maybe three. She hoped Fred would make use of them. She hoped he was praying.

The Bowl Inn, St Giles

Onlookers were crushed at the windows and doors of this tumbledown little tavern, which would do more business in an hour today than in the whole rest of the week. Inside, the prisoners were supping their penultimate drinks, and some of the riflemen had joined them, more to slake their own thirst than keep the crowd at bay. *Fred'll have hot rum*, thought Sarah, remembering how he liked it: spiced with pepper and horseradish as well as cinnamon, nutmeg, cloves. *Hot as the Devil's blood*, he'd always say when she made it for him, and pull her down into his lap, and laugh.

He'd met her in a pub. The other woman, the one whose name Sarah declined to speak and prayed to forget. The one he was on his way to swing for. Not at the Bowl, but the Exmouth Arms, two streets away from their little house in Clerkenwell. What she'd been doing in there who could say; nothing she'd own to in church, Sarah guessed.

Georgiana. A high-sounding name for a low sort of woman. All bouncing bubbies and yellow ringlets, the brazen little bitch. He'd had women before, she wouldn't've minded, but this one was different: expensive taste. Fred couldn't keep up both the households, wife and mistress too, not on a groom's wage, and he chose Georgiana. Sarah would never forgive him that. Not if he beseeched her on the scaffold.

She'd found a haberdasher's bill in his waistcoat pocket, a list of extraordinary, extravagant things: dyed ostrich feathers, yards of silk ribbon, trimmings and beadings and lace. Always leaving things in his pockets, was Fred. Careless, like so many criminals; so many who were caught and hanged, anyhow. She'd said nothing, just left the bill folded neatly under his plate at dinner, so when he'd finished his chop and pushed the plate away he'd seen it, and the look on his face was enough.

He'd left that same night, knowing when the gig was up, having chosen already anyway. A week went by. A fortnight. A month. Still Sarah told nobody he'd left. 'Away on business,' was all the neighbours knew.

One time he came round, two in the morning it must've been, near beat the door down, begging to be taken back. Finally she'd let him in just to shut him up. Georgiana was a devil, a treacherous siren, a villainess, he'd said. He couldn't live with the woman any more. Sarah had folded her arms, said nothing. There he'd sat, weeping into his hot rum, his new blue coat ruined with mud, one pocket flapping loose. Once, she'd have mended that. Now, she gave him a drink and sent him back to his whore.

A week later, Georgiana's pretty head was found tumbling in the Fleet, the rest of her to follow. She'd let Fred keep her and clothe her, it seemed, but wouldn't leave off her other gentlemen. They'd found letters from her in his coat; bloodstained, as was his pocket-book. He said they'd had a fight and she'd gone off, he hadn't seen her for five days before she turned up again, bobbing down the river in bits. Nobody believed him; standing in the dock, he'd hardly looked as if he believed it himself. Dazed, that was the word. Like his old life was a dream he was trying to remember, slipping away.

Sarah, veiled, had sat at the back of the public gallery, imagining he was watching her every time he looked up. The jury took five minutes to find him guilty; the judge only one to settle the black cap on his grey wig and sentence Fred to hang.

A bumptious cheer as the door of the inn opened: two guardsmen stepped out, followed by the prisoners, looking a lot less glum, especially the pea-green silken highwayman, whose powder had sweated off, his face now a shiny strawberry against his suit. Fred came out waving like he was the Prince bloody Regent at a public promenade. In his hand was a pewter tankard of ale. He showed it to the crowd, drained it off and tossed it up, flashing in the sun, to be caught by a kiss-blowing doxy or an idle apprentice. The guards pushed him roughly against the cart, tied his hands back up, tossed him into the straw like a sack. He sat up smiling, his dark wedding-coat dusted with hay, and executed a clumsy bow.

'I'll buy you all a pint on the way back!' he yelled, and a gust of laughter spread through the appreciative audience. Always liked to be liked, did Fred. Always the soul of the party. Quick to laugh, eager to please. She would not, would not cry.

The Mason's Arms, Seymour Place

The last stop, and the prisoners' last drink. Food too, if they could stomach it, though it was hard to eat with one hand manacled to the wall. Sarah felt weak and hungry in the heat herself. She bought two oranges from a street-seller and opened the flesh of one with her pocket-knife, sucking its juice greedily. Another hot rum, for Fred's final drink on Earth. Fresh orange squeezed into the smoking glass gave it a citrusy zing.

Georgiana's last drink had been hot rum, too, made just the way Fred liked it, because Sarah didn't know any other way. She'd turned up the night after he had, in a rain-spattered dress, her fine hat awry, ostrich feathers bent and drooping; the yards of expensive silk ribbon half torn off her skirts and sleeves. Sarah had seen what he saw in her, then; even so dishevelled, she was a rosy, buxom, winsome thing, bursting with youth.

She'd listened quietly, sipping ale, waiting for the powder in Georgiana's rum to take effect, as the girl babbled about how Sarah had to take Fred back, that she was afraid for her life, that she'd done wrong to steal him away. Eventually she stopped talking, and Sarah went to work.

She knew a slaughterman at Smithfield: Fred wasn't the only

one with secrets. He got a guinea for his work and his silence, and she promised more besides, when he cared to stop the night. They couldn't be seen together for a while; not till after Fred's trial, anyway.

Sarah knew there'd be a trial because Fred had left his blue coat at hers, and Georgiana'd had a letter in her gown telling him she was leaving, which she hadn't dared to send. A fingerprick of Sarah's blood over that and the pocketbook, and the coat pushed through an open window for the law to find when she passed Fred's house next day, and it was done.

Tyburn Tree

The gallery was heaving: Sarah strained on tiptoes to watch as the hawkers brandished copies of the 'last dying speeches'. 'Daring Rob' the highwayman's ballad was outselling the Clerkenwell Butcher's, she noticed, and he hadn't even killed anyone. Fame, fickle fame.

Fred stepped up, wearing that same uncertain expression she recalled from their wedding day. The hangman, a hulking fellow all bald head and huge hands, blindfolded and hooded him; his arms were already tied. The pickpockets and horse-stealer had stopped dancing five minutes back, and it was time for the main event. Poor Rob Dare was green as his suit now, and Fred looked about him anxiously, even with the hood on, as though he'd lost something.

For the briefest of instants Sarah wondered if it was her he was looking for, then scoffed at her own foolishness. She stared a second longer, then, as the hangman reached for the lever, averted her eyes.

She heard the slam of the trapdoor, the creak of the stretched ropes and crowd's gasping groan: but all she saw was the heartless blue of the April sky as she turned her face up to the sun, and smiled.

Quarantine

These days, Sy has to be careful. Everything is sealed and sterilised, boiled and disinfected; but caution is a way of life now. Or at least a way of avoiding death.

Sy's building, a twenty-storey edifice of wet grey concrete the colour of angry cloud, is hermetically isolated from its neighbours on the Marylebone Road, which have different contagion indices. The mirrored black structure to the left is occupied by Stage Three Symptomatics and bears the double blue warning lines. The right-hand block is a smaller Victorian building housing asymptomatic Carriers. In a way, these are more dangerous than the S-3s, as they could be mistaken for being Clean; but superstitiously, Sy regards the venerable brick town-house with more affection than the tower of dark glass.

Love, even companionship, is elusive in the current environment. Sy smiles at her reflection. She doesn't aim so high as the poets people are reading again, entranced by tales of knights sworn to serve maidens in high, impregnable towers. Her teeth are even and small, the colour of polished bone. It would be crazy to expect real love, physical love, here and now. Sy rejects the lipstick: red might remind her date of the second, hyper-sanguine stage of Kiehl's syndrome. Not very romantic. Online relationships have increased, but flesh-and-blood partners are a rarity. Concealer over the blue skin beneath her eyes and thin black lines around them. Love is harder than ever. Long hair twisted into a chignon, stabbed tight with a syringe-shaped pin: surgical chic.

Sy's panel burrs. She smacks the button beside the bathroom mirror.

'Yes?'

'CleanCabs confirming your 19.30 booking Miss Terrill S. Please reconfirm.'

Sy pouts and rolls her eyes.

'Reconfirm. No condition change, MedInsure unexpired. Happy?'

'Thank-you Miss Terrill S. Good health.'

It amuses and annoys Sy that although the CleanCabs woman is not a machine, she still chooses to talk like one. Perhaps she feels it might confer some magical immunity from the terrors of organic existence. There's a lot of it about. Cyborgs and the Amended are more visible on the panel shows: entertainment, not news, naturally. News reports are full of suicides and untouchables walking suitless in the plaguey air, too far gone to know or care where they are. Driving through open streets, even in the sterilised taxi tanks, is discouraged unless strictly necessary. The roads are eerily empty; the wide West End pavements and lofty arcades of the City full of cardboard tenements. Fires leap from oil drums in winter; corrupted, semi-naked bodies lie prostrate in the heat of summer. Thrill-seekers go down among the dispossessed sometimes; tooled-up lone stalkers, slumming it for a nihilistic buzz. Suited functionaries, garbage men and post office workers, still perform the basic municipal tasks, except that nowadays they are armed. Not that the sick and dying can do much to an integrated suit, but without armour or weaponry, the paranoia can get you before the untouchables do.

The panel tinkles the news sponsors' signature tune, and Jace Gohan's warm, plastic tones ooze out. He is Amended: you can hardly tell unless you look closely, but under the studio lights his skin has a nacreous sheen and his third eyelids flicker momentarily when he looks down. Sy gets a little twinge in her belly whenever she sees this: the Amended are more than human, removed from all the dirt and vulnerability humanity implies. Cleanliness is sexy: words like *machine* and *vacuum* have become erotically charged since the disease's spread. The obsession with hygiene started as a necessity and has become a fetish. All the breaking porn stars are Amended; a few are cyborgs too. Smooth sharp contours; total efficiency. The Amended aspire to be angels, and in another generation or so, science and the panel shows whisper, they will be half-way there. Not for the first time, Sy wishes her parents had amended her. She could have been almost invulnerable, almost indestructible; almost perfect. She studies the black sweep of her eyeliner, the gold on her lids: today she is wearing 1969. Almost perfect.

Sy can't remember the last time she left her building, let alone saw the streets. Perhaps it had been for her mother's funeral; but even then, the windows of the hired limousine had been mirrored on the inside. The car had told her it was so the bereaved didn't get upset. Sy had turned away from her distorted reflection, wondering what could be more distressing than the deformed iteration of her face that stared back at her, oozing down the curved glass like a tear.

They stop once beside a statue of Eros, who leans half-cocked from his platform, bent and battered in the Celibacy Riots of ten years ago. Sy's heart throbs unevenly as on the edge of her vision, something pale limps along the gutter. Sy panics before realising it's just the wind fooling with a discarded sterile glove. Its plastic is torn but it still waves white at her from the side of the road. She imagines the horror of losing sterility, of the diseased air surging over skin and into lungs: of knowing you will never be Clean again. It must be like drowning. Sy checks her biomonitor, but it blinks normal.

A bar flashes past as the cab starts up again. The windows are bright, bulletproof, full of light; the people inside are twisted by the curve and thickness of the glass as they shoot coy glances at themselves to an audience of empty streets. Mirrored on the inside. The stripes on the sign are white, Clean. So many all together, a vivarium of the rarest, most endangered species.

The barman mixing her cocktail is suitless, obsequious, understatedly handsome. The bar is underground, a wide white room that, with the appropriate codes, leads into the once-famous restaurant behind. Sy has arrived half an hour early, unaware and uncaring that the traditional female entrance must be made late and loud if at all. She and a few uneasy-looking couples are the only occupants: the décor is laboratory and her cocktail arrives in a Pyrex container marked with fluid measures. Every time they hear the swoosh of the bar's airlock over the glassy background music, everyone whips round ferally to observe the new arrival. The bar's sweeper system excludes those who do not belong: the blue-stripers, the contagious yellows. Sy is claustrophobic: a pair of bare-skulled women in surgical greens are far too close, exchanging gossip and sly, charged glances at the next table but one. Sy heads abruptly for the bathroom to take her pills: calm, contraceptive, and the other one. She hopes they will not kiss: lesbianism doesn't disturb her but physical contact does. The last human being Sy touched was her dead mother: the latex of her glove as she stroked the cold cheek had left a ghost of white powder on the corpse's skin. She had not died of the disease, unusually, but the funeral director had murmured through his mask that Sy was better safe than sorry.

Alex sits at the counter, still as his own photograph. Unusually, he hadn't sent the standard 3D download, but a black-and-white digitised headshot, like an actor might use. He and Sy had messaged at first: once, he had phoned her, but she hated the barren silences that swooped in on them like vultures in the middle of conversations. She is used to listening, not speaking: her words come out of hiding in their own sweet time.

His profile is old-fashioned, like one of the retro cocktails they mix here: a sharp nose and chin, very black hair, a reassuring starburst of smile lines around the eyes. The music is louder, or her ears have adjusted to the bathroom's silence, and she can barely hear her own voice as she says his name hesitantly, like a password. He doesn't turn round. In the angle of the bar mirror he studies the few lone women guarding tables for two with ferocious hope. Though it's more difficult for men to catch the disease, it hits them faster and harder, and once they have it they always die sooner. There aren't many healthy ones left. Half the couples in the bar are female. Despite government breeding incentives it's not children women want these days: just someone with whom not to have them.

He searches for Sy's face, for he has seen her just as she has him, through a glass darkly: he's looking for his tower-trapped maiden, his pure princess. Her breathing is fast and shallow as a bird's as she taps his shoulder, and extends her hand to shake, lowering her eyes to a point a fraction below his own. Even through her gloves his hand when he grips hers has an unsettling warmth.

They are served in their decontaminated and sealed-off booth, by a human waiter who looks like Jace Gohan and seems to Sy's trained eye as though he too might be Amended. The thought warms her chest as no amount of Alex's smiling and careful compliments can. She is not sure what in him she distrusts, as he flicks carelessly, bare-fingered, through the leather menus (why aren't they laminated? Sy does not remove her gloves) and talks about his work: something worthy, forgettable. He asks about her job and she tells him she works from home (who doesn't?) for the Department of Statistics, monitoring population, demographics, rates of birth, marriage and death, contagion indices. She doesn't tell him that always beneath the ebb and flow of numbers and the staggering ascent of graph lines she can sense, almost see, the disease moving like a shark underwater; like a worm beneath skin.

He smiles at her and says it must be interesting.

They order. She's used to home-cooking, an old-fashioned skill her mother taught her, which she indulges partly out of respect for the dead and partly to make the long hours of the lonely day go faster. She orders only vegetables tonight: although in theory animals cannot be carriers, she has seen the rise of the disease, the blue stripes lapping at her door like waves, and she doesn't know how not to be afraid. One of the things that attracted her to Alex, allowed her to imagine his monochrome face opposite hers at the breakfast table, on the sofa, perhaps even in the bed, was that he too chafed against the institutionalised fear: found it more pathological than the disease itself. Sy is not superstitious or ignorant: she knows the exact figures and is still afraid and hates herself for it. Even the calm pill has not dampened her anxiety enough to stop her shrinking instinctively from the touch of uncovered skin, or allow her to eat meat in a strange place.

They both start at the hiss of decontaminant in booth's atrium, but it is only the pearl-skinned waiter with their starters. As he slips them onto the glass table Sy studies his hands: they are smooth and impregnable as latex. Amended skin is difficult to tear or break, a far better first line of defence against pathogens than mere evolution could have designed.

Alex orders champagne. She isn't sure whether to be charmed by his impulsiveness or a little alarmed by it. He is not cautious, but perhaps that is a good thing? Sy revolves the concept in her head. Looked at logically, three-dimensionally, if he is what she is not, if he is up to her down and vice-versa, might they not complement each other better? She imagines them fitting together as neatly as protein and receptor: two pieces of the same biological jigsaw. The calm pill's effects seem to be enhanced by the champagne: she meets Alex's eye and begins to see that, unlike Gohan's sincere, all-embracing gaze, his is hers alone. It is the closest to closeness she has felt since her mother, and at last it is not like looking into the dead eye of a mirror.

She is relaxed enough to smile as she decants her with-alcohol capsule: she would have popped it with the others but hadn't thought they would be drinking. Alcohol mixed with her usual regimen of drugs has unpredictable, unpleasant side-effects: the capsule negates them, for a few hours at least. He smiles back but doesn't produce a matching container, nor ask for a pill. Sy is puzzled: to drink unprotected is more than incautious, it's reckless.

'Where are yours?' she asks. He shakes his head gently.

'No need.'

'What do you mean?' The agency had promised it would never match her with anyone on alternative therapy or at an advanced, drug-impervious stage. She feels her throat closing up and the pill lodges in her throat, its soluble plastic case slowly melting. Blue stripes shiver before her eyes. She who has been so careful. No.

He smiles again and pulls his contagion indices out of his shirt, a gesture as blatant and shocking as stripping naked in the vacant streets. Her own indices, the dogtags hidden between her breasts, are striped like a barber's pole with the red of remission. His are a blank slate: stripeless white.

She leaps up and backs away, cringing as far into the corner of the room as she can. Tears clutch at her choked throat. She yells at him, incoherently, to go away, to stay away. He stares and does not move.

She had been so cautious, chosen the place so prudently: pleasant, discreet, remitters only. No. Remitters or above: what would be the point in refusing a Clean client, if they chose to come in? Because no-one Clean and in their right mind would choose to, of course. She thinks of their hour in the booth, together alone, breathing one another's air, her infected words entering at ear and mouth, at eye and wound, his blood dirtying with the disease.

She opens her eyes and he is almost on her, his Clean fingers brushing her face. She flinches violently and shrieks. The booth is soundproofed by a walled vacuum for the sake of privacy and hygiene.

'I wanted to meet you,' says Alex, as though it were the simplest and most obvious thing in the world for people to meet in person and like each other and touch mouth to mouth at the end of the night, like some Hollywood fantasy from the last century. His hand touches her cheek, hot to her cold skin as fever. She has no breath left to scream: she gasps and shudders. She looks at him with the hate and despair of a trapped and tricked animal, the despair and hate of the dying for the suicide.

'You're Clean,' she spits.

'I'm not afraid.' He strokes her cheek. She imagines a ghost of white on a corpse's skin. 'Not if you're not.'

But she is.

The Nuisance

She always knows when it is about to start. A few days before, she will notice the little twinges that presage the nuisance – a stitch in her side, cramps and coldness in her fingers; a heavy, bloated feeling as though her body is too full of blood. The warning signs are unpleasant and leave her fractious and snappish, but at least they give her time to shop and prepare. The nuisance needs a surprising amount of preparation, especially if she's to keep it private and carry on as normal. It's almost a relief when it comes. It leaves her drained; clean and empty. Safe again for a little while.

Ever since it began, she has read as much as she can find on the subject, interrogating the internet, making her way to the upper room of the local bookshop, getting funny looks at the library. It seems that for most people, it happens predictably, regularly, and it goes on for years. Hers seems to adhere to no schedule – at least so far. She comforts herself, tentatively, with the thought that perhaps it's like getting your period; haphazard at first, before it settles down and regulates itself. Perhaps the others hadn't gone public until they knew when to expect it? That would make sense. No use alerting the press if you weren't damn sure you'd have something to show them.

Fortunately she always rises before James, especially when the nuisance is on its way. It's a working habit she can't seem to break, even though since Mattie started going to nursery school she's home alone all day, with nothing but paperwork and housework to do. But she's always been a lark. James, a night-owl who thinks nothing of reading in bed until two in the morning, can't understand it, hiding his head under a pillow as soon as her bedside lamp goes on at six.

She showers, cleanses, and brushes her teeth, then pads down to the kitchen in her bed socks. She makes toast and tea and pours cereal, calls Mattie down, and the two of them eat together at the tiny breakfast bar while Daddy is theoretically showering and shaving, although sometimes he barters cleanliness for an extra half-hour in bed. James shambles down the stairs at a quarter to eight, grabs a low-calorie oat bar to eat in the car, and takes Mattie to nursery and himself to the station. She sits quite motionless, for five or ten minutes at a stretch sometimes, after waving them goodbye. Then she sweeps the crumbs on the table into the cupped scoop of her hand, loads the dishwasher with dirty things, and pours herself the last cup of tea in the pot.

This morning, the new blank time hangs heavy on her, like wet clothes. She wipes the surfaces and thinks about watering the garden, but when she peers through the Venetian blinds she sees that it is raining. She walks slowly upstairs to dress for her expedition to the shops. She chooses clean old jeans, a white t-shirt and a long navy sweater. Her hair is bundled into a cap, to keep the rain off; she wears sensible black boots. She does not exchange her glasses for contact lenses, or bother with make-up; she wants to be invisible today, now she knows the nuisance is looming.

There are three chemists in town, all in the centre, which is a fifteen-minute walk, mostly beside a busy arterial road. She tries to alternate her visits to them in case any one of them starts to wonder. The narrow footpath is bordered by tall tangled hedges, which shed their weight of rain onto her brushing umbrella. The dull tap and patter of raindrops on the taut nylon depresses her. She always tells people she loves it when it's raining, but she doesn't really; what she loves is to sit inside, her chair pushed up against a warm radiator, and watch it fall.

Today she needs a box of surgical gloves, new verruca socks, more plaster and gauze, the eczema cream she never uses, and perfume. She goes to Beynon's, where the girl behind the counter is new, and fills her basket first with the sort of staples they can always find a use for; disposable razors, shower gel, toilet paper and nappies for Mattie, just in case. Then she locates the other items and tucks them inconspicuously underneath the Andrex. She needn't have worried; the girl swipes everything through with comatose efficiency and processes her card, never once taking her eyes off the arrestingly handsome young man who is browsing near the door. She thinks she recognises him, but isn't quite sure; she lowers her eyes and edges past him. He does not move or acknowledge her. She is relieved.

In the coffee shop she buys a latte and sits at the tiny table in the window, and watches the rain. Rain changes people's body language, even their walking pace. The shelterless slouch into their collars, those with umbrellas are pert as meerkats, scanning the pavement for potential clashes. Nobody walks normally through rain; they either trudge or scurry. She notices the young man from the chemist's, black hair slicked to his wet cheekbones. He's the exception, striding like a hiker through the pedestrian crowds. She still can't slot him into a category. She's not good with faces. Where does she know him from?

She sorts through her purchases and opens the box of gloves, bundling a pair in her jeans pocket just in case, along with a couple of large plasters and some cotton wool. It almost always starts overnight, so that she has to rush off and attend to herself the minute she wakes, but she has been caught out in the daytime once or twice before. Although she can feel the nuisance approaching inside her, as she might see a thunder cloud on the horizon, there is just no way to tell how near it is until the storm breaks. A silly analogy, she thinks, stirring her coffee. It's really nothing like as dramatic as a thunderstorm.

She leaves money and a tip in the saucer and makes her way to the Ladies'. It's almost lunchtime; she should get home and start cooking the dinner. Her habit is to prepare everything in advance and have a small portion for herself for lunch. It's boring for her to eat the same meal twice a day, but it saves some effort – although what she is saving her energy for these days, she does not know.

Washing her hands, she realises it has started. The tap runs pink into the basin, and thin threads of blood, like dark spittle, swirl in the water vanishing, down the plughole. She dries her hands on paper towels, wrapping them like a boxer's fists, trying to blot it as fast as it appears. She rummages in her jeans pocket with her paper-bandaged left hand, searching for plasters, and finds the surgical gloves, slippery with powder. She lays them on top of her handbag and sticks large square plasters over the bleeding backs of her hands. Then she wads cotton wool into her palms, which are always worse, securing it with plaster strips. She notices herself sweating in the stale lemony overhead light. Somebody knocks on the door; it has a note of restrained urgency.

'Just a second!' she says, her voice high and polite, like someone in a sitcom. She puts the thin, translucent gloves on over the dressings, bins the debris of wrappings and bloodied paper towels, takes out the black leather gloves she always keeps at the bottom of her bag and pulls them over her fattened hands. She fluffs her hair in the mirror, picks up her bags and unlocks the door, apologetic grin fixed. A blonde woman barges past, a small boy following, his hand pressed between his legs. The door bangs behind her.

She leans against it for a moment and rummages in the chemist's bag for the perfume. She spritzes herself liberally; it's cheap, no-brand stuff and she hates its brassy, floral scent, but it disguises the smell. She hopes she will be all right until she gets home, as it's the first day and she's got the rubber gloves on underneath the leather, but her chest might start seeping like last time and she doesn't want to take any chances. She thinks of her old white t-shirt underneath the navy sweater; never mind, it can be washed or given to Humana.

It's too wet and she is in too much of a hurry to walk back; she flags a taxi down at the bottom of the hill and gives her address. The grizzled driver makes a face at having to go such a short distance, and another, equally unpleasant one when her gloved, clumsy hands fumble his fare, but anything's better than walking. At home, she can feel safe; swab the wounds, examine the damage, dress them properly with cream and thin absorbent gauze and, most importantly, make herself a cup of tea. If she's lucky, her feet and side won't start bleeding until the second day. For some reason, the hands always come first.

She stumbles in through the door, keys shaking in her hand. Sometimes, when the nuisance is coming, she gets dizziness, too, and fleeting pinpoint headaches. This is one of those times. She heads for the kettle and peels off her outer gloves with trepidation as she waits for it to boil. The dressings underneath the thin white rubber are still clean, apart from two bright blotches of red at their centres. They'll be good for another couple of hours. She remembers with a rush of relief that James has somebody's leaving do this evening; he won't be home until late. Plenty of time to make preparations, in case it's not just the hands that start tonight. She pours her tea and sits at the kitchen window, balancing the mug on top of the radiator to keep it warm. The rain has stopped and the garden outside is dripping, striped and spangled with afternoon sun. She has an hour before she has to pick up Mattie from nursery; preparing the dinner can wait.

Upstairs, she takes the maroon towels from their place at the back of the airing cupboard. In the bathroom, she removes the dressings and plasters and flushes them down the toilet before stripping completely and stepping into the tepid bath. Hot water increases the bleeding. Slender trails of red snake from her pale hands, distorted through the angle of the water, but she soaps and scrubs as best she can. Once she has dried herself on the dark towels, she stands naked in front of the long mirror to examine her whole body in the hard white light.

Hands first; the wounds are still superficial but are bleeding freely, if more lightly now. They will only get worse; she'll probably need some more gauze before it's over. She slaps a couple of small plasters on them to stem the flow while she looks over the rest of her. She doesn't want to mess up the bathroom floor. In the mirror, she watches herself narrowly as she lifts up her left arm, then her right, as though for a breast exam, running her fingers along the spaces between the stretched ribs, feeling for a gap or cleft.

The chest wound has appeared twice so far, each time on a different side, as though trying to work out where it ought to be. The holes in her palms have once or twice migrated to the base of her hands, almost at the junction of the wrist. Fortunately, that was in November; she had bought long faux-suede gloves which James had admired. She can feel and see no break in the skin, but she will wear her black thermal vest under her pyjamas tonight just in case. She bends abruptly at the waist to stare at her feet. There is still worn pink polish on her toenails from drinks with Tom and Wendy last Saturday; she grabs cotton wool pads and nail varnish remover and rubs the ragged remainder off while she examines her soles minutely.

The left foot is clear but the right is beginning to rupture, and smudges red on the floorboards as she lifts it to check, wobbling on one leg like a dazed flamingo. For safety's sake, she hops to sit on the closed lid of the toilet where she bandages both feet, top and bottom, opens the verruca socks and drags them on, pulling her normal socks over them. No tights or open-toed shoes for a few days. Both feet will probably be showing the injuries by morning; she remembers the depressing squelch of a sock full of blood from last time. Panty-pads work best to line them, but it's difficult to fiddle them in.

She checks her watch and dresses again in double-time; only fifteen minutes before she has to collect Mattie. No time to call a taxi, and anyway Mattie doesn't like changes in his routine;

she'll walk, as usual. The pain in her feet won't start properly until tomorrow, if she's lucky. The plasters on her hands will have to do; she slips an extra layer of cotton wool under the surgical gloves and puts the leather ones back on. Her fingers are already stiff and slow; she has a suspicion that if she held her naked palms up to the strong overhead bulb, she would already be able to see a drop of light through them.

At the nursery gates one of the other mothers asks her where she got her gloves.

'You've always got such lovely accessories,' she says, and twinkles her rings in goodbye.

She and Mattie make fairy cakes and watch television all afternoon. Mattie loves her black gloves, petting and stroking the soft calfskin and trying to pull them off finger by finger when she's not paying attention. He's seen them before but is always fascinated when they appear. Mummy's magic hands, she calls them, and pretends she can perform spells when she has them on. The spell for the afternoon is making the cakes come out perfectly, which they do, and making the rain, which has started again, stop so that they can play football in the garden. As the sun sinks, they venture out for their game and Mattie's faith in magic is restored.

While he is napping she calls James to find out if he will be home in time for dinner; he tells her he will grab something at the station. To soak up the booze, she thinks, and smiles. Mattie and she have a special treat for dinner; a shared ready meal from the freezer drawer. After she's read him to sleep, she curls up like a fox on the sofa and tries to watch television, but she's bored and restless; she switches off as soon as the news comes on. James will be home soon, and her hands are hurting properly now. Upstairs, she takes the painkillers and eczema cream from the bathroom cabinet, swallowing the pills with a gulp of water from the tap and setting the jar of cream on the bedside cabinet like a stage prop, so that James will see it when they go to bed. She reperfumes herself and swaps her black leather gloves for the white cotton ones she keeps in the cabinet's book drawer. They look formal and faintly ridiculous; her conjuror's gloves, James calls them.

She is in bed, the light out, by the time he gets back. He smells pleasantly of beer and peppermint as he reaches for her, but she places her gloved hand over his and resettles it around her waist. He registers the layers of pyjamas and vest.

'Cold tonight?' he murmurs. She nods and hears her hair sigh on the pillow.

'I'll keep you warm,' he says, already on the edge of dropping off, and spoons himself around her, his erection subsiding. The noise of the night rain keeps her up for a while, staring blankly at the streetlit curtains, but eventually she joins him in sleep.

The gash in her side appears the next evening, and despite swaddling herself in gauze and tight bandages, blood seeps into her blue pyjamas overnight. Fortunately she sleeps on her back and it doesn't stain the sheets. Once James and Mattie are gone for the day, she hand washes them awkwardly, made clumsy by the Marigolds over her plaster-stiff hands, using the last of the Vanish. She takes out her black silk nightdress and lays it on her pillow, then opens her dressing-gown to see how bad it's got. Peeling off the bandages is almost always an unpleasant surprise.

The thick, sweet flowery smell emanating from her open flesh is overpowering, brash and heady like wisteria, and the hole is wider and deeper than before; she's never seen it so bad. Fascinated, she advances the tip of a gloved pinkie and pushes it into the wound. Blood flows sluggishly over the surgical latex. The pain is sharp and dull all at once; a rasping buzz when she touches it, a sucking ache when she removes her finger. Her headache is back, too; it feels like her skull is in a studded vice. Ibuprofen barely damps it, and she has moved onto Migraleve.

She catches herself grimacing in the mirror; she tries to unscrew her face but the lines of pain stay. And there are what look like bruises on her forehead. She shuffles closer to the mirror; she can barely walk at the moment; her tiptoeing, painful steps give her away. The verruca socks squish and squeak.

Around her brow, at regular intervals, are tiny bleeding cuts, little tears in the skin like the marks made by barbed wire. She wipes the blood away with a Kleenex, brushes her thick fringe down over her forehead, and calls the doctor.

'Dr. Mitchell is ready for you, Mrs. Denton,' says the nurse. She looks up sharply; she hadn't really been listening on the phone when she made the appointment, concerned only to see someone as soon as possible.

'Isn't Dr. Chandra in today?'

The nurse smiles patiently. 'She's on a course. Don't worry, Dr. Mitchell's new but he's very nice. He doesn't bite.'

'Oh,' she says, looking at her fat leather hands clasped in her lap. 'All right then.'

Dr. Mitchell is very nice, and very young, or so she thinks when she knocks timidly and enters his office. He's bent at the sink, washing his hands; dark longish hair, a regular, handsome profile. She recognises the brand of the latex gloves in the box at the side of the basin. When he straightens to face her she realises that he is also the man she half-recognised in the chemist and then the street a few days ago. Of course; she has seen him once before, last September, when Mattie had a throat infection. He smiles and she stares at his even white teeth.

'Well, Mrs. Denton,' he says, 'how can I help you?'

She doesn't know what to say. She starts unbuttoning her black silk blouse, gloved fingers clumsy; his eyebrows rise but he remains calm, professional, holding her gaze. Under her bra a rough white bandage circles her chest. A thick pad of cotton wool, criss-crossed by flesh-pink plaster, bulges beneath it, just below her left breast. Blood is already showing through in spots, brash bright scarlet, like lipstick.

'I've tried to dress it myself but I'm not an expert,' she says. 'I thought you might have something …'

He stands up and moves around the desk to take a closer look.

'First of all, how and when did you do this, Mrs. Denton?'

She drops her eyes. 'A few days ago. It didn't bleed much at first but now it keeps soaking through.'

He looks into her face, hard. He has wide dark brown eyes, to match his hair.

'And how? If I may ask?'

She has been dreading this. Part of the reason she delayed seeing anyone about it until now is that she cannot think of a convincing lie. The wound looks as though it has been made by a blade of some sort, but a wide, dull one; not a knife. Perhaps a sharp rock? Or closed scissors? She shakes her head and says helplessly, 'I don't know.'

He frowns and moves closer.

'You must know, Mrs. Denton.'

'It wasn't anyone else,' she says quickly, 'and it wasn't me either.'

He looks puzzled. 'Are you telling me it was an accident?'

'Yes,' she says. He holds her gaze for a second, then looks back down at her bandaged ribs.

'I'd like to have a look at the injury,' he says. She climbs onto his examination couch without being asked and lies back on the cold green vinyl. Her eyes are tightly closed as he snips off the bandages and carefully peels away the sticking plaster and cotton wool.

'Sorry about the smell,' she says. A hot tear escapes from her screwed-up eyelids and travels down her cheek. Fortunately it's on the side away from him. His cool fingers dance around the open edge of the wound, gently prodding and probing. It seems to hurt less when he touches it than when she does, she thinks, trying to control her humiliated urge to cry. Perhaps it's because he's a doctor.

'Don't worry,' he says, confusion rising in his voice, 'it's not gangrenous. There's no infection. In fact, the wound looks very clean. When did you say it happened?'

She swallows dryly. 'Two days ago.'

'What penetrated the skin? Was it metal?'

'I don't know,' she says, lying desperately. 'I just fell over. In the garage. The light blew and I stumbled. There's all sorts of stuff in there.'

'Hmm,' he says. 'Maybe garden shears or something.'

'Yes,' she says, with relief. 'Maybe.'

'When was your last tetanus jab?'

She shakes her head. 'I'm not sure.'

'Better have another one.'

'Will I need stitches?' she asks. Perhaps if he sews it up it will heal in a normal way and that would fix it. But then again, who's to say that it will appear in the same place next time?

'You should be ok,' he says. 'It looks like it's healing pretty fast already.'

She glances down fearfully, but to her astonishment he is right. The gash is already visibly smaller than it was this morning, as though it is withdrawing back into her body, disappearing without leaving so much as a scab or a scar. The injuries always heal themselves seamlessly, eventually, but she has never known it happen so swiftly before. Could it be his hands, his doctor's touch? She dresses again and submits to the tetanus injection; the serum feels heavy and cool, like liquid metal, and her arm aches as it enters her veins. The needle leaves a tiny violet bruise on her arm, but no blood. He smiles.

'If there's anything at all you'd like to tell me, Mrs. Denton,' he says quietly, 'about your injury, or … well anything –'

'No,' she says, 'thank you.' He nods in defeat.

As she rises to leave he offers his hand; she has no choice

but to shake it. He can feel the padding in her gloved palm, she sees it in his eyes. He glances down at their joined hands; she disengages quickly and picks up her handbag.

'If this happens again,' he says sternly, 'this or anything like it, I would like you to come straight to me. I'm always willing to discuss … anything you'd like to share.'

'Thank you,' she says, and leaves. Her gloves slip on the handle as she tries to turn it; he steps forward and opens it for her.

'Goodbye Mrs. Denton,' says Dr. Mitchell, 'I hope we don't need to see each other again.'

When she gets home, James is watching a programme on TV about the Turin Shroud, Mattie sprawled on his lap.

'How was Dr. Chandra?' he asks.

'Not there. I had a new doctor. Mitchell or something.'

'Is that the hot one Lucy-with-the-twins keeps going on about?' asks James with mild interest.

'I suppose so.' She sits down and presses a wrist into her aching brow. It comes away with a pinprick pattern of blood spots. When she returns from the bathroom, the presenter is talking about whipping and crucifixion.

'Turn it over,' she says shortly. James, a fan of *The Da Vinci Code*, protests.

'It's horrible stuff for Mattie to watch,' she says. 'Morbid.' She takes the remote and changes the channel at random, to a noirish police drama.

'You think this is more suitable for a three-year-old?' asks James dryly.

'It's well past his bedtime anyway,' she says, and scoops Mattie brusquely into her arms to take him upstairs. She doesn't come down again.

That night, as James slips quietly in beside her, she reaches out her arms and clutches him violently to her, shivering in her pyjamas.

'I love you,' she whispers, 'I love you.'

'What are you scared of, conjuror girl?' he asks, his voice soft with sleep. He squeezes her cotton-gloved hands affectionately. She's glad that it's dark, and he can't see her wince.

She doesn't go back to Dr. Mitchell for two months. It is neither difficult nor easy. But when the head wounds come back as she knew they must, they are deeper and there are more of them. She can't wash her hair; she can barely walk or use her hands. James, noticing the spread of what she still tells him is eczema, keeps mentioning a dermatologist he knows. Eventually she agrees to see the doctor. This time she asks specifically for Dr. Mitchell. She comforts herself that professional ethics will prevent him from revealing anything she tells or shows him to anyone else; patient/doctor confidentiality is like the seal of the confessional; that she knows. She is sure there must be something else he can do to help her. She has always had great faith in medical science.

'Is there … much pain?'

Dr. Mitchell sounds like there is something caught in his throat. She lies on his examination couch, shirtless, hands and feet naked and dripping. Blood spots the thick rough hygiene paper she lies on, as on a sheet. She shrugs and winces; the chest wound has reappeared in a spot further around her body, almost on her back this time. It makes it harder to see and dress the cut. She wonders how much stitches would hurt.

'The pain's doable,' she says. She smiles up at the ceiling. 'Nothing compared to childbirth, anyway. Mostly, I take Ibuprofen and try to ignore it.'

'You mustn't,' says Dr. Mitchell quietly, 'you mustn't ignore it. How can you ignore it?'

She sits up carefully, twisting on her good side.

'I have to,' she says. 'What else can I do?'

He strips off his surgical gloves and drops them in the bin at his side.

'Well,' he says. 'There you have me. The wounds are clean – apparently self-cleaning, they don't get infected or suppurate. You said that they heal rapidly of their own accord in a few days?'

'Yes,' she says. 'When they're at their worst, they – well, you've seen it. I can push my little finger right through my palm, or in between my ribs. But after a bit they just disappear.'

'Completely?'

'Completely. Until the next time. No marks, no scars. It'd be easier if there were; that way I couldn't keep tricking myself that I'm imagining the whole thing.' She stares at her perforated hands, clasped tight to minimise the trickling.

'Well,' says Dr. Mitchell, 'although you certainly lose quite a bit of blood over that time, you don't seem to suffer any ill-effects from it – except of course the pain and nuisance of the injuries themselves.'

'Nuisance,' she echoes. He shakes his head.

'I'm sorry, poor choice of words. I'm well aware it's much more than that.'

She looks carefully at his face at he goes to fetch something from behind his desk. He looks young and handsome and tired. Almost as tired as she does. His hair needs cutting. There are swags of shadow beneath his eyes.

'Won't you sit down, Mrs. Denton?' he says, nodding at the chair. She dons her rubber socks and gloves before pulling her wraparound top on carefully and tying it at her waist. She sits in the patient's chair opposite him. He has opened a large, square hardback book, the glossy, photographic kind that sits unread on reception-room tables the world over. Even upside-down, she can see what the picture is. Even without looking at his face, she knows what he is going to say. He rotates the book so that she can see the image; a double-page colour spread of pale flesh and blood, painted to look real.

'Do you know what this is?' he asks gently.

'It's not that,' she says.

'Mrs. Denton, I –'

'I'm not Catholic,' she says vehemently. 'I'm not religious at all. This has nothing to do with that.'

'I know how ... odd it seems, but to be honest I'm not sure it can be anything else.'

'Why not?' she asks. He looks right at her, absorbing her fierce gaze, calculating.

'I suppose you have done your own research on this,' he says, 'and so you know what the indications are. The spontaneous appearance and disappearance, the pattern and nature of the injuries ... even the scent, the ... perfume they give off.'

'Even if it was that,' she says, 'would it make any difference? Could you cure me?'

He taps his lips lightly with a finger.

'No,' he says, 'I suppose not. It seems like yours is a condition which needs to be ... managed, rather than cured.'

'Then will you help me?' she says.

On the first Friday in April she collapses, screaming and bleeding, while preparing lunch. Thank God neither Mattie nor James is home, is the first thing she thinks when she comes round, her cheek pressed to the cold kitchen tile. She staggers to the phone and calls Dr. Mitchell, and then the taxi firm. She has an account with them now. To them, she's the lady with the bad feet.

Dr. Mitchell is firm and exasperated when he sees her. His mouth is grim as he washes her bleeding feet and inspects the wounds, his head bent intently so that his long fringe tickles her toes. He disinfects, dresses and binds her hands and side; he dabs tiny flesh-coloured plasters in a line across her forehead and winds a bandage around her head. She protests but he insists.

'Wear that cap of yours,' he says brusquely, 'if you still want to hide this from your family.'

'Thank you,' she says. She is still lying on the couch, foetal on her side. She feels terribly weak and peaceful, too languid to get up. He scrubs his hands fiercely at the sink, his angry back to her. He turns and contemplates her for a moment, then he goes to the wall and lifts a five-year calendar down from it.

'Do you know what a red-letter day is?' he asks. She shrugs and shakes her head.

'A special day?'

'Yes.' He is marking something on the calendar in biro, scribbling furiously in his elegant, illegible doctor's hand. 'But the original reason they were marked in red was that they were religious holidays. Saint's days, holy days, and so on.'

He turns the calendar around to face her. She lifts her head a little, but it's very heavy. She stares at the calendar sideways on. It's the page for last August. There is a thick blue scrawl over a red-blocked square.

'The first date you said this happened,' he says. He flips over two pages; a different date this time, but again the blue and red coincide.

'The second time. November. Notice anything?' She nods wearily. He flips to December; a thick blue circle around the last few days of the month. He flips again.

'January. The first time you came to see me.'

A blue loop encloses a red square. Flip.

'Our second appointment.' She is no longer looking; she gazes up at the porous ceiling tiles and hopes they don't contain asbestos. She hears the slick slap of turning pages.

'Today. Do you still say that this is nothing to do with what I showed you?'

She remembers that awful documentary James had been watching after she came back from Dr. Mitchell the first time. Nails in the hands and feet. Thorns in the scalp. A spear jabbed into the ribs. She closes her eyes and feels tears slide between the lids. She turns onto her other side, her wounded side. She hears his footsteps on the lino, feels his hand on her shoulder.

'This is not a curse,' he says calmly. 'This is a gift. A gift you should share.'

'I don't want anyone to know,' she says. Her tears are muffled in her hands but she knows he can hear them in her voice. He sighs and passes her a Kleenex.

'How about your husband?'

She shakes her head and sniffles.

'He doesn't know.'

'But the gloves … What do you say to him?'

She smiles at the wall.

'I say it's eczema. I had it as a child,' she adds, as though that somehow makes the lie true.

'You can't go on hiding this,' he says firmly.

'Yes,' she says, 'I can.'

'But why, for goodness' sake?'

She knows how mad, how maddening she must seem. But not half as mad as she would if she let her secret out. She turns to face him, composing herself, scrubbing the tears fiercely from her cheeks.

'I don't want to be seen as a weirdo, Dr. Mitchell,' she says. 'Or a liar, or a freak. If I tell anyone about this – if you do – everyone will think I'm crazy, or a charlatan.'

He's staring at her at though she's already talking nonsense. His eyes are wide and shining, full of something – pity, or fear, or both.

'Don't you see?' he says. 'This is a miracle.'

He takes the crumpled tissue from her clenched, bandaged fingers and spreads it out before her eyes, like a white-gloved conjuror. It is stained with blood where she has been crying. She raises her swathed hands to her eyes and starts to laugh.

'Let me show you something,' he says sharply. 'Maybe this'll make you understand.'

He pulls her hands away from her eyes. He's holding a plastic box, which he places gently in her lap. Inside the box are smaller boxes, each labelled and dated. They contain swabs of cotton wool, plasters and bandages; they look like the collection of an obsessive hoarder, or an abrasion fetishist.

'What on earth is this?'

'These are all from your second appointment, two months ago. When you showed me the full extent of your … injuries. I kept them just in case.'

'You did what?'

He is flushed with determination; he pulls a Perspex box out and gives it to her.

'Open it.'

'What? No!'

He yanks it from her and opens the lid himself. Inside lies a loop of bandage with a spreading bloodstain.

'Two months ago, right? The blood should have dried long ago but it looks fresh, doesn't it?'

She peers closer, disgusted and fascinated; it does look fresh. Bright and arterial, as though it had just that moment left her body. Dr. Mitchell touches a trembling finger to the bandage, and it comes away sticky and red.

'It is fresh,' he says. 'And they're all like that.' He stares at her with the yearning, straining gaze of an animal, willing her to follow him.

'This is a miracle,' he says. 'You are a miracle.'

'I have to go,' she says, gritting her teeth with the pain as she sits up on the couch.

'I've got someone I'd like you to meet,' says Dr. Mitchell rapidly. 'Perhaps at our next appointment? A friend from the church. A very clever man. He might be able to help you.'

She stops. 'Help me?'

'Yes,'

'Can he stop it?'

Dr. Mitchell looks away, spreads his hands. 'Help you come to terms with this. Understand it. Accept it, even. Maybe.'

'I see.'

'Please think about it.'

She nods, avoiding his eyes, and limps out.

A few weeks later she is feeling much better. Sometimes, when she wakes up in the mornings, there are a few blissful moments when she forgets the whole thing. She is getting better at conning herself that it's all been a hysterical dream. Mattie is with her on a visit to the chemist's for the first time in ages. Mr. Beynon greets her with pleasure.

'Nice to see you back, Mrs. Denton. We've missed you.'

She smiles past him and hurries away. When she gets home there is a message blinking on the answering machine. Mattie's nursery, probably.

'Mrs. Denton,' says the voice of Dr. Mitchell. 'Sorry to call you at home. Just wondering whether you've had any recurrence of the condition? I was rather expecting to see you in here today. Could you give me a call?'

She sends Mattie upstairs and dials the number. He answers immediately, sounding flustered.

'It's me,' she says. She realises how conspiratorial she sounds. She realises that she doesn't even know his first name. He knows hers, of course; but to him she is always, respectfully, Mrs. Denton.

'I'm glad to hear from you,' he says.

'I got your message. Is today a red letter day?'

'Yes,' he says. 'Are you coming in?'

She doesn't answer.

'Have you thought any more about meeting my friend? He could –'

'It's stopped,' she interrupts. There is a shocked silence. When he speaks again he sounds incredulous, and a little indignant.

'Stopped? Everything?'

She nods, clears her throat.

'All of it. No bleeding, not even any pain. Just gone.'

'Are you sure?' he says quietly. He sounds far away, and lost, and sad. Or perhaps it's the echo on the line.

'I'm sure,' she says. 'It's the sort of thing you know. It's gone away.' He doesn't answer. 'Thank you for all your help,' she says, 'but I won't be coming in again.'

There is a pause, then,

'Thank you,' he says. 'Thank you.'

The line at his end goes dead.

Mattie's voice floats down from the landing; he wants a story, or perhaps a toy, she'll go and see. She puts the phone down gently and sighs. She gets a Kleenex out of the box beside the Yellow Pages and wipes a bright smear of blood from the receiver, balling the tissue into the palm of her hand. Then she goes upstairs.

The Co-respondent

She bought a third-class ticket at Victoria and sat looking determinedly out of the window all the way down. She watched her new hat and frightened eyes ghost in and out of wet green trees and livid grey sky in the glass. By East Grinstead, she'd bitten the unfamiliar paint off her lips, and had to wobble her way to the ladies' room to reapply it.

When she sat back down, the little boy opposite stopped pinching his mother for a spell, to ask why that lady's mouth was so red. He wore a peaked grey cap and short trousers of the same dull, hardy fabric: he could not have been more than seven. His mother, a dowdy, harried blonde with roots showing, looked up sharply and then drew her feet in by an inch so that they might not touch Abigail's patent-leather toes. The heels were new, too, bought to match the hat, at the promise of her first paying job in the new business. They weren't the sort of shoes Abigail would normally wear: too obvious and bright; common, really. And the three-inch heels were impractical for waitressing. She tried to take the mother's surreptitious glances of disapproval as a compliment: she must look like what she was meant to be.

When she emerged from the smoke and fuss of the station at the top of the hill, for a second she wanted terribly to go inside again at once and board the first train back to London. Either that, or rush down the hill in her tart's shoes straight into the sparkling sea, which looked, for that brief moment, blue and inviting beyond the mint-green Victorian railings and the marbled pebble beach. Then the clouds drew their dusty net-curtains across the sun again, and the shine went off the water, like a Birmingham ring rubbed dull.

The Sea View Hotel was at the bottom of the hill, on a side-street; a view of the sea obtainable only by putting one's head out of a third-floor window and craning. But Abigail wasn't there for sight-seeing, and neither was he, so she supposed it didn't matter. She signed the register with slow care, trying to write neatly and remember the correct spelling. Her gloves made her clumsy; she noticed an ink-stain on the left thumb. She took them off and stuffed them in her hand-bag sheepishly. She ought to have bought a new pair of those, too. No earthly point in doing anything half-way – that was what Elsie said. It was Elsie who'd got her into this. Easy money, she'd said. Five pounds for half a day – more than they got in a week at the Lyons' Corner House, including tips. Bloody Elsie. Abigail felt like boxing her ears, now: her stomach was trembling and she felt thirsty and sick under the clerk's oily gaze. But the only thing to do was push through. Onwards and upwards.

The clerk took the pen back from her with fastidious fingers. With a wry jink to his eyebrow and a glance at her naked ring finger, he told her that 'Mr Smyth' was waiting in Room 203. Blast! Why had she taken her gloves off? Little fool! She balled her hands into fists as she stepped into the elevator, avoiding the eyes of the smirking bell-boy.

'Second floor,' she said, too loudly, and he touched his cap and pulled the gate across, getting a good sidelong look at her legs as he did. She was used to men's casual glances at work, but in the tea-room at least they waited until her back was turned. She'd had to slap away a few pinching hands, but it wasn't like this: the customers didn't take her for cheap, only poor. At least there was dignity and honesty in poverty. Again, she regretted taking up Elsie's offer, so fiercely it brought tears to her eyes; but it was too late now.

She was reminded of why she'd said yes when the bell-boy stopped outside Room 203 and looked at her expectantly. She smiled with a flash of desperation, and rummaged fruitlessly in her bag, knowing it contained nothing except a few hair-pins and the green paperback she'd been too nervous to read. 'I'm awfully sorry,' she said. 'Perhaps when...?'

He shrugged his indifference. 'At least you ain't got no bags,' he said, significantly. His eyes lingered on her red mouth; then he was gone. She pressed her lips together then rubbed her teeth with a finger, pinched her cheeks, shook her curls, and knocked. The noise was loud and dead in the dingy, carpeted corridor. She wondered for a brief, alarmed moment whether she ought to put her gloves back on, then the door was jerked open and there was a gush of pale afternoon light, blocked by the dark silhouette of a man.

'Hullo,' he said.

'Hullo,' she replied.

He took her in for a second, then stepped back to allow her to pass into the room. He had dark hair slicked back with Brylcreem; it was melting already, and a lock had fallen over his pale forehead. He was smoking a cigarette and wore a navy-blue double-breasted suit with wide shoulders and a chalk stripe. She hadn't really known what she'd expected until she saw him in the watery light of the worn hotel-room, and he wasn't it. She'd thought he might look beastly, somehow, or caddish, or like the sort of spiv who sometimes came into the Corner House late in the afternoon when everyone else was back at work, who chewed on a toothpick and was overly familiar and always under-tipped. But he didn't look like that at all.

The room was mostly pink: the faded upholstery was the colour of face-powder, the counterpane a slippery, satiny salmon, the carpet a bold shade of blown rose, trodden dark. Mr Smyth gestured her towards the window, as far from the double-bed in the corner as possible. She was determined to ignore the bed's existence, as she might ignore a rude or flirtatious remark to which she had no answer. There were two old-fashioned high-backed chairs, and a sort of low tea-table with an ashtray on it which looked crystal and was likely glass; the large, heavy sort people bludgeoned one another with in green paperbacks.

Beyond the table was a dirty sash window, and beyond that a red brick wall with a faded advertisement for Brasso. Beyond that hung a sky full of rain. The rain was whispering drearily against the glass and she felt a draught from somewhere and heard a faint rattle, and for a second it was so horribly real and sad that she wished she could scream, or cry. But that wouldn't do anyone any good. She was here to do a job and the client didn't want a silly girl bursting into tears on him. That was exactly the sort of thing Elsie had said she must avoid.

'Strictly professional, strictly small-talk,' she'd said, carelessly, through a mouth full of pins, as she fussed with her hair. Gareth was waiting at table 12 for her to come off shift; he was taking her dancing at the Trocadero. That was why Elsie had asked Abigail to go instead.

It was easy work, though fearfully dull, Elsie had said: she'd been doing it for a year or two now, on and off. When people got divorced adultery had to be 'proved' against one or other of them, she'd explained – even if nobody had done anything. It was considered the gentlemanly thing for the husband to allow himself to be named as the guilty party, and the best way to arrange this was to take a hotel room with another woman in as obvious a manner as possible. Brighton was the best place for it – handy for London, and plenty of hotels. Sometimes the word of the desk clerk and the porter was enough; sometimes there were Pinkerton types taking photographs. She'd made it sound rather exciting.

'Think of it as a day out,' Elsie had told her. 'You don't have to be nice to them: just civil. It's all they expect and in most cases, more than they deserve.' She'd removed the last pin from her mouth and replaced it with her cigarette, which she'd left burning in the dry soap-dish. Then she'd kissed Abigail on the cheek, leaving a hard red mark, and fluttered her fingers in goodbye.

'Thanks awfully for doing this, darling Abby. You're a brick!'

Mr Smyth followed her to the table and watched anxiously until she sat down, hovering as if he were waiting to take her order. She smiled. He smiled. His teeth were even and very white. He stabbed his cigarette out in the bludgeon-ashtray, which already contained four or five crumpled butts. He couldn't have been here more than a quarter of an hour. The room had been booked for two p.m. and she had only been a few minutes late.

'You're Edith, I suppose?' he said. There was something about his accent; it sounded exotic, mid-Atlantic, like a film star's, but wasn't, quite.

She shook her head. 'Agnes. Edith couldn't come.' Always keep the same initial, Elsie had said: it was easier to remember. Your name doesn't need to be real, Elsie had said, any more than his does. It's the photographs that matter. She wondered where the detective was lurking: on the street outside in the rain; in the foyer, waiting to catch them – perhaps even in the hotel corridor, just beyond the door? She cast a fearful glance behind Mr Smyth and he half-turned.

'It's OK,' he said, in that odd accent of his, like someone pretending to be American, 'nobody's gonna disturb us. Nothing to worry about.' It sounded like 'a boat'.

'You're Canadian!' she said suddenly, forgetting herself. Her aunt's husband was Canadian: he had been a pilot in the War. Mr Smyth smiled in a cautious sort of way.

'No flies on you, I guess, Agnes,' he said. 'Care for a drink?'

She very much cared for a drink but didn't know if it would be professional to accept. She looked around for clues: a half-drained whisky tumbler – real crystal this time – sat on the sideboard, alongside a chrome ice-bucket and tongs.

'I'm having one,' he said encouragingly, and followed her gaze with his feet, crossing to the sideboard, picking up and draining his drink. 'Or rather, another. We've two hours to get through, after all, and there isn't much else to do. Join me?'

The way he said it she knew he wanted it more than most

men wanted a kiss or a win on the horses. She could hold her liquor, as long as it was only a little: where was the harm?

'All right,' she said, and he smiled again, wider now, all teeth and crinkled eyes. When he wasn't smiling you could see the ghosts of where his crows'-feet were, white lines in the sunburn. Though his build was wiry rather than muscular, he looked healthy and outdoorish, somehow; like he ought to be striding along the seafront or riding a horse, not cooped up in a dingy pink room with a perfect stranger. He looked as if he'd never been in a hotel like this in his life, and she was fairly sure he never had.

'On the rocks?' he asked. An ice-cube was clamped in the tongs held over her glass. She nodded: it splashed. He handed her the tumbler and clanked it with his own.

'What shall we drink to?' he asked her, as he sat down. She shook her head. She didn't want to suggest the King: it seemed somehow disrespectful, under the circumstances.

He crinkled his eyes again and laughed silently. 'Here's to divorce,' he said, slapping a chalk-striped knee. He drank half and set his glass down. She sipped hers; still too strong. The melting ice made oily swirls in the brass-coloured liquid. She put it down and looked out of the window for something to do. Perhaps there was a pack of cards somewhere? She should have thought to bring one. They could have played Patience – though that was a game for one, of course. She racked her brain for card-games innocent of the taint of gambling, but could only think of Snap.

'Done this before?' he asked her. His voice was quieter now, as if the whisky had soaked into it, damped it down. She shook her head again.

'Me either,' he said. He reached into his breast pocket. She thought suddenly, absurdly, of gangsters and revolvers, and flinched – but he only brought out a silver cigarette case and flipped it open, offering her the sole remaining cigarette inside.

'I can't take your last,' she said. 'I must have some, somewhere.'

Elsie had given her half a packet yesterday, when she'd finally run out of money except for the price of her train ticket. She'd gone hungry this morning, without even a few pence for a cup of tea and a bun. She'd rather have had a sandwich than whisky and cigarettes, but it seemed rude to impose. He was spending enough on her as it was.

'Don't worry,' he said, 'I'm not pulling a Gordon Comstock. I have plenty more.'

'Gordon who?' Perhaps he was a Canadian film star? Comstock, that was, not Mr Smyth.

'A guy in a book. Forget it. Take one,' he urged, shaking the diamond-patterned case at her. She did. He clicked a matching lighter and held it out for her to take the flame at her tip. As she leaned in she noticed a web of silver scars on his knuckles and a worn inscription on the lighter: To Peter, With Love, From – the name was obscured.

'Is it a good book?' she said, to keep from wondering about the name.

'It's OK. Pretty funny.' He shrugged. 'Pretty sad, too. All about a guy who thinks he's too poor to fall in love, kind of.'

'What's that to do with cigarettes?'

Mr Smyth smiled a painful small smile. 'The guy has a trick – keeps a single cigarette in a battered old packet and offers it to people at parties. They all say 'Oh, I can't possibly take your last one – have one of mine!''

Abigail thought she might remember that ruse, if she were a man: it was clever, and a little sordid. Luckily, any girl worth looking at never needed to carry her own.

'You can tell the author's British,' Mr Smyth said, peering out of the window into the street below, as if trying to spot somebody. 'This is the only place in the world it'd work.'

She laughed politely; then, because he looked like he expected more, she wondered aloud what sort of man wrote books like that.

'One who's been poor, for sure,' said Mr Smyth thoughtfully.

Outside, the rain was now pelting down as if it meant business, as though it had something to say to the sea and the town and all the people in it. She turned her wrist ever so slightly and glanced at her watch. Only ten minutes. More than a hundred to go.

'Speaking of which,' he said, and darted swiftly back to the sideboard, on which she now saw a black leather wallet. She looked away quickly, but he had already grabbed it and was taking out and carefully unfolding a large white five-pound note.

'Just so you know I'm good for it,' he said, waving it like a little flag. She didn't want to touch it: it made everything seem too real. He looked around for somewhere to put it down; finally he brought the whisky decanter over and put it on top of the note, like a paperweight. She got up as he set it down, clutching her hardly-touched glass.

'Is there any soda?'

'Sure, help yourself,' he said, gesturing to the sideboard. She found the siphon and topped up her tumbler, almost to the brim. She took a gulp with her back to him – it tasted weaker and sweetish now – and felt better, then turned to face him again. He was staring at the end of his cigarette, watching it burn between his fingers without smoking it. He had a nice face; lean and even, with eyes which were slate-blue in the afternoon light. He was about thirty, she supposed, clean-shaven, brown-haired – though he might be dark blond without the Brylcreem. He didn't look like a Peter. All the Peters she had known had been bluff hearty chaps with donkey voices, like big schoolboys. She wondered what he did for a living. His fingers were long and elegant. Perhaps he was a pianist, or a painter.

Suddenly he looked up and caught her staring. She felt a fiery flush lick her cheeks.

'Wondering how anyone could divorce this matinee idol, right?' His mouth quirked. He tossed off the whisky and trickled a little more into his glass. 'Well, she's got a better offer, it seems. Some Scottish guy. Lives in a castle, maybe even owns it. Been running around with him for about a year. I travel a lot for business, so I ... didn't notice. Should have. That's what she said. That if I'd've noticed she'd have thrown him over. But I didn't, so she wants a divorce. But she doesn't want the stain on her character, and neither does he, so here we are.'

Abigail just looked at him, thinking about the invisible name on the lighter. Elsie had not told her what to say when the small talk ran dry. She licked her lips and drank more whisky-and-soda. The glass was getting empty. There were red stains on the rim where her lipstick had smeared off. She must look a fright.

'You look a little like her, you know,' said Mr Smyth, with something between sadness and amusement in his voice. 'What does that mean, I wonder?'

Abigail didn't know. He had put a paper packet of Senior Service on the table between them and she darted forward like a bird to take one. If she smoked she wouldn't have to talk – that was how the film stars did it: Garbo, Mae West, they just smouldered and were silent. He looked full into her eyes for the first time as he lit her cigarette, just for a second, and then looked away again like he was ashamed.

'At least it's credible that I'd be making time with you,' he said. 'Young and pretty, hair and figure like Iris. My friend Don, he had to go through the same charade for his wife and the agency sent a dame who looked like the Ancient Mariner. Can you imagine?' He sat up straighter and a gleeful gleam came into his face. 'The jury actually laughed when they saw the photographs of the two of them coming out of the hotel together. Wonderful talker, apparently. She spend the whole time showing him photographs of her grandchildren and offering him toffees out of her purse.'

He gestured to the whisky decanter. 'This is all I can offer, I'm afraid. Unless you'd like a sandwich, or something? You look a little pale, there. I can ring for room service?'

She shook her head defiantly, as her stomach yawned with

hunger. He cocked his head. 'Are you sure?' She didn't trust herself to answer; was afraid that if she opened her mouth a great gurgle would surge out, betraying her.

'OK,' he said slowly, 'call me crazy, but you're only a slip of a thing and I don't like to see a girl drink on an empty stomach, even if it is only soda water. I'm gonna get us a little something, OK? No need to eat it if you don't like, but I don't want you fainting on me or anything, or thinking I'm the sort of guy who'd really get a girl in a hotel room like this, with nothing but whisky on the menu.'

The bell-boy came in five minutes, with a carelessly-made doorstep of white bread and ham, and some pickled onions on the side. Mr Smyth jumped up at the knock. Before he opened the door he pulled the salmon coverlet off the bed and peeled back the blankets.

'For appearances' sake,' he apologised. He took the plate at the door and gave the bell-boy two shillings; she could see the tip changing hands from where she was sitting, but the boy couldn't see in. He probably imagined her sprawled on the invisible bed in a silk negligee, *in flagrante delicto* – was that the phrase? Abigail remembered that Americans and Canadians were always generous tippers. Perhaps that was why she'd liked his voice from the first.

Mr Smyth came towards her with the sandwich and she couldn't pretend any more. He watched her as she ate. He had started diluting his whisky with his soda now. He wouldn't even take a pickled onion. 'Hate the things,' he said with a grin. He talked a little while she ate – mostly about Donald, his friend whose wife had divorced him, too. They'd been in the War together, in France. Donald lived in Battersea and had a nice new girl now, a stenographer. Donald said getting divorced was rather like having a leg off – after the initial shock, it wasn't so bad.

When she'd finished her sandwich he said, 'Enough of me,

Agnes. We got an hour. Tell me about yourself. You can make it up or you can lie, I don't care. But we might as well talk.'

She told him some lies and some truth, and some things which were in between. She said she modelled clothes for one of the fashion houses on Sloane Street, which was half true because she had, before she'd got too thin for Madame Aubade. She said her parents were dead, which they might as well be. She doubled her number of boyfriends to four, but said there had been nobody serious: he looked pleased at that, even though it might have been a lie for all he knew. She jumped when the clock on the mantel dinged four p.m., and looked at Mr Smyth. She felt dreadfully selfish, having talked about herself for a whole hour. What must he think of her? Suddenly she was embarrassed again; he must want her out of here now it was all over. Now that everyone had seen them together and could swear to things in court, she had done her job and could leave. She stood up too fast and her head swam, despite the sandwich. She pulled on her gloves hastily, wincing at the ink-stain.

'Well,' she said, absurdly, 'thank you for a lovely afternoon. And the sandwich.' She stuck out her hand, shook briskly, and started to hurry away.

'Wait,' he said when she had her hand on the doorknob. There was a tinge of amusement in his movie-star voice. 'Where are you going in such a rush?' She turned, horribly afraid. She thought of girls lured to places like this, doors locked quietly when they weren't looking. She looked at him, dreading what she might see. She had thought he was so nice. Elsie had said – curse Elsie!

He was holding up the five-pound note quizzically. 'You'll need this, won't you?'

She nodded. She felt hideous to think such things of him. He was just a nice man whose wife wanted to get rid of him, who had to go through all this just so adultery could be proved against him. She wanted to tell him she was sorry for him. She wanted to push the lick of hair that fell over his brow back into place, so that he didn't look so scruffy and sad all of a sudden.

She shook her head.

His eyebrows drew together in puzzlement. 'What?'

'Keep it,' she said very quickly so that she couldn't change her mind. 'Spend it on ... on ... a nice girl, like Donald's. Take her to the – the Trocadero. I can't take it, I'm sorry. I'm not cut out for this. Thank you for the sandwich.'

She tried to open the door but the handle was stiff and her gloves were slippery with sweat. He lowered the note and folded it again, neatly, like a napkin.

'I would,' he said, 'if I thought I could find a girl as nice as you. But I don't even know your real name.'

She looked at him. Peter. He had his hands in his pockets and he looked like a man she'd once seen, leaning in a doorway on the other side of the road from the café, staring up at the smog-coloured moon and smoking a cigarette in silence, smiling. She had always wondered what that man had been thinking.

'There's a girl I know,' she said at last, 'who has rather a pash for Canadians.'

'She has good taste,' he said, thoughtfully. 'We're nice folks.'

'She works in the Lyons Corner House on Dean Street, Soho,' she said. She looked at him seriously. 'You might want to write this down?'

He tapped his head. 'No need. Go on. What's her name?'

She folded her arms. 'Tell me where she works, again?'

'Lyons Corner House, Dean Street, Soho,' he repeated.

'You'll do,' she said. 'Ask for Abigail.'

She walked out of the hotel and smiled at the rude bellboy and the insinuating clerk. There was no detective outside, but she wouldn't have minded if there had been. She stuffed her stained gloves in a public bin. She wouldn't be wearing them again; she couldn't afford to buy new ones, either, not without that five pounds, but she didn't care. Her heart was beating like the sea against the promenade as she ran up the hill in her absurd patent-leather heels, and the sky, at last, was blue.

Sarah James

The Trouble With Honey

As we sit down, Lizzie's eyes dart around the diner with its yellowed plastic surfaces. She opens her mouth slightly as if to test the air for splinters. Finding none, she smiles at me.

'It's been a long time,' I venture.

'Yeah.' Lizzie looks around again, still perched on the seat-edge. Her smile deflates almost as quickly as it curved upwards – like a trace of sunshine glinting on metal: a flash, then gone.

'So, what have you been up to?'

'I.T. work, from home. I don't go out much.'

'Interesting job?' I ask, noticing that Lizzie's face is almost as pale as the cream in her iced latte. Her skin is still smooth as a magnolia petal, her long hair the colour of alfalfa honey. She's as pretty as she was, if in a more subdued way.

'I code from my room. Mum sees to clothes and food. Home delivery.' Her voice stretches every syllable to a high-pitch whine.

'You still get ill?'

'Not often. Mum says it's fine, so long as I don't go out.' Her eyes fidget; fingers cling to sterile wipes, feel for her EpiPen. Earlier, I'd caught the scowl on her mum's face as she looked at me as if assessing my threat risk. Then she double-checked that the pen was in her daughter's bag, and asked again if we wouldn't be better staying in and having a drink there...

'You don't go out at all?' I ask Lizzie, still trying to reconcile this version of my friend with the one from my memory.

'Not often. Mum worries.'

'About the bees? Or new allergies?'

'The bees.' Lizzie's gaze flits from table to table, diner to diner, shadow to shadow.

'But it's winter...'

'Yeah, but Mum says it starts with one thing, and then another. She stays in with me.'

'I guess.' I follow my once best friend's eyes around the room, try to picture how it must seem to her, every clink of metal or crockery the sound of danger swarming.

'Are you back for long?' she asks, and I hear a trace of the old warmth, of the Lizzie before her Dad left, before the broken hive, when we were still close.

'A week or so.' The air between us vibrates with unvoiced questions. Was it this bad before I left for London? How come I never realised? Sure, I'd heard whispers, dismissed it as gossip – we'd drifted... Even so, why hadn't I checked?

'It's a real treat to see you. Glad we came out.' The words drip awkwardly from Lizzie's mouth, as she stares at the warning bracelet chaining her wrist.

'Me too.' I remember how hard I'd had to press to get her to agree, and once agreed, to get her out of the house. My cappuccino is still half-full and so creamy that it churns my stomach. I gulp down another mouthful. 'I'm getting married in July, would be lovely if you'd come?'

'Sure. Congratulations, Kim! That's marvellous.' Lizzie's eyes sparkle momentarily, then the light disappears. I wonder if she's weighing up what safeguards she'd need to be outside in the summer. 'I'm still single. Some male friends online, but we've never met up. Mum worries about the germs, the allergies if we kissed, or something...' Our eyes meet for a second, then hers dance away. 'It's not worth the risk...'

'Maybe you could make my hen party?' I gulp down another mouthful of my coffee. 'Or a quiet drink at my parents'...meet Tim's friends, perhaps?'

'Hmm...'

'He's coming here with his best man on Sunday...' I'm not sure now if it's guilt, nostalgia or pity driving me to push this, while I've got the chance, while she's on her own.

'That's very kind, Kim, but…'

Lizzie's phone buzzes, and she jolts to her feet, knocking her glass. Her undrunk drink slops.

'Time to go!' Lizzie exclaims sharply, as she reads her text. 'Mum's worried.'

I imagine a queen bee piping nervously, calling her only daughter to her side. Then I look at the sudden brightness in Lizzie's face after reading her mum's message. For the first time since we reached the diner, her eyes are alive, lit up by the attention, eager to get back home to their hive.

Our Skinny Dragon

'Can you feel her?' I shriek to Paul.

There's no answer, just the dark cave and eerie shadows where my helmet light bounces off cold rock. My fists clench, memories helter-skelter.

*

'Can you feel her?'

My tone is so different the first time I ask this, holding Paul's hand to my belly where our skinny dragon is flexing her wings. I watch his eyes widen and spark, as he too feels our daughter's fiery dance.

The name 'skinny dragon' comes from Paul's first words of surprise at her fluttering shape on the ultrasound screen, like flames and wings. Somehow, it fits better than the real names we discuss, then reject.

*

'Can you feel her?' Paul's cry to me, fifteen weeks later.
'No!'
'Are you sure, Em?'
'Noooo!'

Our voices flint and strike against each other, as the duty midwife moves her stethoscope and prepares to page a doctor.

Then, found again at last, her heartbeat like tiny explosive dragon breaths.

*

'Can you feel her?'

The incubator is a plastic cage. We take it in turns to stroke Fi's hand clenched tight, and tiny as a muesli cluster. Every flicker of muscle, every movement of her chest is a little lightning strike, our own breaths trailing behind hers like spent matches. When

Paul sings to her at night, his lullaby is as much for us as Fi, struggling to fill her lungs.

Finally, the day that I hold her in my arms, as much skinny caterpillar as baby flame-thrower.

*

'Can you feel her?' I scream again now, as I see light emerging from the back of the cave.

'Yes! They've got her.' Paul's voice is breathless, exhausted, but loud.

'My God! She's okay?'

'Rock fall blocked the main exit. But they managed to find another crevice and Fi was thin enough to wriggle through.'

And there she is, pale-faced, cold and muddy, silver-blanketed on a stretcher.

'Mum?'

'Yes, love, I'm here.' I stroke a straggling hair from her cheek.

She thrusts her hand into mine – my skinny dragon: forcing us again to catch our breath, her body fuelled with fire.

Not Running

'Have you … talked to Simon?' My voice gusts onto the winter air like unsteady cartoon speech bubbles as I try to run and chat.

'Thursday, when he's back.' Cath has no trouble balancing breath and words.

'You have…to tell him…about Ben.'

'I guess.' Cath's voice is vibrant, too vibrant. But I don't have chance to probe; my words are few, gasped.

Fifteen minutes into our usual route, it starts to snow. Small cold kisses at first, but ten minutes later the path is layered white. Distant trees become pastel lines then disappear into sky.

We turn back. Our pace slows from jaunty jog to dragging slog. My face is numb. Even Cath stops talking. She brushes a hair from her eyes. Her sleeve falls down, revealing new bruises.

She catches my glance. Her expression says, 'It's nothing'. I disagree, but now's not a time for questions. The path has turned into one long white treadmill. We concentrate on each step, raising our feet like mechanical pistons, pushing against the wind, barely moving.

Eventually, we reach Cath's house. Dark and empty. She closes the door and I shock her hall into light.

'Rodney the monkey is having a fit and may be more ill than the park keeper thought...' Someone has left the television booming in the living room. Sometimes, it's Cath's son, Ben, gone out in a rush. Other times, she leaves it on for company when Ben's with his dad, Simon.

We flop, shivering, onto chairs. The kitchen fills with our breathing and the agitated monkeys' distant screeching.

I look across at Cath, and her bruised wrist.

'Thursday. I'll tell Simon about Ben on Thursday.' Cath

sounds so definite, but I see her arm tremble.

'Oh Cath!'

She looks up, her eyes the colour of the morning's sky just before the snow fell. Then she turns away.

'He's my son, Mel. My son.'

Out Of The Box

It was a stupid place to hide, Jess realised afterwards, but Carl's magician's box was open when she heard his footsteps on the laminate. She already had his mobile, had wiped his hard drive and should have been on her way out...

It was dark inside the box – Jess sucked in her breath – darker than their nightly audiences could ever have guessed. Carl's footsteps stopped. Perhaps he had discovered his handkerchiefs that she'd hacked to pieces, or the rabbits' hutch, its door now swinging open, the straw inside empty. She should never have trusted a man who could saw a woman in half, call her 'my bunny'; then pin her against the wall. Their 'magic' wouldn't have lasted longer than five seconds if he hadn't taken those pictures, and held them over her.

'Jess, is that you?'

She heard him kick the table and cursed herself again.

'I'll get you, Jess!'

Footsteps again: louder, closer...then silence.

Jess exhaled softly, hoping Carl had reached the spot where he'd see through the doorway to his reflection in the bedroom mirror, and his favourite suit freshly dry-cleaned, a love note pinned to the collar. With its 'My great Majestico...' and the promise of a night of passion, surely, he wouldn't resist.

She heard the bedroom door slam, calculated in her head: at least five minutes smoothing the jacket and eyeing himself up. Jess climbed quietly out of the box and headed towards the back door. Another two minutes before Carl tried his trousers, and found that she'd specially altered them. Then thirty seconds more maybe before he realised her note had a few home truths on the back. It was almost a pity she couldn't stay to watch the show, but Kelly would be waiting, her long dark hair scented with citrus fruit, her skin and lips glossy from the shower…

Jess picked up her suitcase from the doorstep and headed down the side path towards the taxi that pulled up as if on cue, to complete her vanishing act.

The Last Red Cherry

Kis pulls the shiniest bauble from the Christmas tree and cups it in her hands. It looks like a see-through planet plucked from her porthole, and, valued at 1000 e-bits, it's the most expensive decoration on the fake fir. Even before Kis had it priced, she knew this instinctively – this crystal sphere is the only thing she's ever seen that is filled with clear water.

Kis switches her gaze from the bauble to the pale honey-coloured liquid that she's been sipping. The glass on her desk is simultaneously half-full and half-empty, even in artificial gravity. She tries to imagine again what Earth water would taste like, how rain would feel on her skin. But Earth is millions of miles away, smaller in her telescope than the decorations on the tree. So small that, if Kis could pick the Earth out of the sky, it would make a perfect necklace bead.

When she was younger and healthier, Kis's great-great-great-grandma used to joke that, from this distance, her home planet was the size of an Earth cherry. She'd also loved decorating the tree every year: with each bauble, a memory or anecdote.

'They did a good job with what they had,' Granchy would tell her. 'This fir almost smells like the real thing!'

'Yes?' Kis smiled.

'That red globe there is the size of a perfect Earth apple – another fruit that's unforgettable, though I can't describe it exactly. So many types and flavours. You'd have to taste one to know.'

Sometimes Granchy would stop there. Other times, she'd talk about the farm where she grew up, with cornfields, grass and orchards. Every summer, she'd scrump fruits from her nan's trees: plums, pears, apples, and cherries. Cherries sweeter than Saturn honey, redder than Mars, the colour of pure, fully oxygenated blood, the last rare forbidden fruit. Kis' mouth waters at the thought of this wonderful thing that she'll never get to taste. Only one such tree left in the solar system, its precise location lost.

Still, at least Kis has this aluminium tinsel tree. If Granchy could see her now, she'd joke that Kis was eyeing up the decorations as Earth women used to drool over displays in jewellers' windows, picking out the rings with the biggest sparkling rocks.

Kis finds it hard to imagine getting excited about hard stone. Metal and mineral are everywhere. Her fascinations are different. Yes, almost everything about the baubles is artificial, but not quite. She's had them tested. Her oldest pieces carry traces of Earth elements, of land dust, even water and once-living matter. Their light and shine too is crafted by hand and imagination in memory of the old ways, in honour of life.

Kis' favourite decorations are the transparent spheres dating from just before the exodus, with scenes depicted inside like mythic hanging snow globes or old-fashioned crystal balls into the future. Granchy used to stare at them for hours before finally pronouncing her predictions.

Granchy's last insight though had been little more than a babbling of random words: 'Honey-river-stone-hail-red-petals-glaze-falling.'

'Falling.' Granchy had repeated the word again before falling back against her pillow in the spaceship sick bay.

Every time Kis visited, she'd look round the small dorm with sinking despair. It was full of patients like Granchy – after centuries of anaemic life, their hearts petal-thin and their minds finally running out of space for more memories.

No point dwelling on this, Kis drags her thoughts back to the fir. She can feel Granchy with her, like the Ghost of Christmas Past, plucking another glass ball from the green branches, then telling Kis to look inside if she wants to divine the future.

But the sphere in Kis' hands is black as a starless night. There are beautiful chiming bells inside but they only sound when shaken. Kis pushes the swinging bauble harder and harder until…the black ribbon snaps and it falls from the tree.

Perhaps Granchy isn't with her after all. Granchy would never choose such a dark future. Kis' hand hovers above a globe with a frozen lake. Brightly scarved skaters dance across the surface to a swirl of beautiful soft yet joyful choral music, its song composed entirely from snatches of different people's laughter. She longs to cradle it in her hands, but she fears this choice. It's as if the Ghost of Other People's Promises is beguiling her with sham dreams.

She touches the next sphere gently – it's entirely filled with flurries of plastic snow – a gift of Christmas Present. The white flakes will not settle long enough for there to be anything but blizzard. Like the cosmic debris constantly pelting the spaceship.

Kis picks up the original bauble again. Granchy called this 'The Rain Globe', saying it reminded her of her last days on Earth. As Kis' other plans seem to have failed, she wonders if she should get Granchy's poem about it framed for Christmas. She flicks through Granchy's e-note until she finds the words.

The Rain Globe

Imagine the Earth sealed in curved glass,
our world as a rain dome. The wet

more frightening than drops of light
glistening towards dice houses.

Hold this sphere in your palm,
turn it upside down and it's the sky

that drowns. Foundations cling
to the thin land above.

Imagine we're tiny people,
speaking through bubbles,

all of us now divers
thrown in water flight,

lives tilted
towards spillage.

But suppose this Christmas is Granchy's last? It isn't the most
cheerful gift to give her, even if Granchy's mind has gone too far
to understand the sadness.

Ting! Kis's electroscreen flashes with a new message.

'Your merchandise has been located. Your order is in g-flight!'

Kis senses her heart pumping redder and faster as she
reads. She'd not really expected her search to work. But now this
message from Galaxis. What if this is it? Finally.

Of course, Kis tries to slow her breathing, it could be a fake –
black-world sellers are notoriously unreliable. But as past-dealers
go, Galaxis' reputation is legendary on the contraband scene. If
it really is a cherry from that last tree? If the rumours are correct,
one sniff may be all it takes to save Granchy.

And the price? Kis wills herself not to think about that,
as she packages up The Rain Globe in stellarwrap. So long as this
works, it will be worth it. It's not the first heirloom they've had
to sacrifice, and she still has Granchy's poems.

Kis hears her own nails tapping the desk in time with her
heartbeat, as she waits for her exchange to process. The noise
reminds her of Granchy's recordings of an old analogue clock
ticking, only faster, more arrhythmic, hollower.

To occupy her fingers and thoughts, Kis turns to one of the

brighter entries from Granchy's journal and forces herself to concentrate on the lines.

Underwater: Surviving

In our new place / the fish
that pour from the tap
rise a little faster \ bubble bigger

Away from town streets / the water
tastes clearer / easier to swallow
unthickened by twists of pipe

through terraces submerged
in the flood \ of their own debris
At sea in this new world

we are strangers to ourselves
Oceans teach us to dive deeper
to find strength we never knew

If…when dry land returns
we will welcome free-walking
but guard tails and fins in case

We made this house of gills
layered with synthetic scales
now \ we swim with it

Although it's the hundredth time Kis has read the poem, this still seems worlds away from her own life. No water, no individual homes on the Interstar, only an infinity of space outside and the increasingly more cramped crampedness of near-communal living inside. But the title and Granchy's determination... survival Kis gets. Survival is the one essential that they've all been fed and watered on. Survival and hope.

Ting! 'Your g-pod has landed!' The electromessage flashes a brighter blue neon than the lights on the Christmas tree, its chime louder than any bells Kis would ever wish for her frozen-lake skaters.

Although Kis is trying to stay realistic, she can't help feeling expectation rise inside her as the small pod arrives in her cubicle-chute.

She prises the pod apart and takes out a tiny box.

It looks the right size. She imagines the weight is right. But she's scared now to open it. She's never seen a real cherry, so how can she even tell if it's genuine? There's only one person Kis knows who will know for sure. The same person that Kis needs it for.

Shoving the box in her pocket, Kis grabs the next zip-express and hurries though the shafts towards the sick bay.

It's hard to distinguish Granchy's dark curls from the shadows on her pillow. Except the shadows are dancing and Granchy's hair and head are still. Granchy's breathing is slower and shallower even since Kis's last visit.

'Granchy,' Kis whispers. 'It's me.'

Kis sees Granchy's eyelids flutter and bends over to kiss her great-great-great-grandma's moon-pale cheek.

'Look, I've brought you something.'

Opening the box, Kis lifts out the waxy fruit by its stalk. This thin wiriness bends with the weight of the shiny soft bead that she's been promised is a real cherry. It looks real, feels it too. She wishes Granchy's eyes would open, and stay open long enough to look, check and reassure Kis.

Steadying the fruit with her gloved palm, Kis uses a scalpel to nick its surface, then slides a tiny sliver of reddish flesh into her specimen dish. If this is what it should be – and if it does what it should do – there's enough cells for her to sample and re-synthesise.

Then, clasping the rest of the small bead gently between two fingers, Kis holds what she believes is the last red cherry to Granchy's lips... and hopes.

Cassandra
Passarelli

Waiting Room

Stepping in from the noise and chaos of the street, Julia took in the rows of plastic chairs; the front ones occupied by women, the ones at the back by men, like church. They faced the altar; the secretary's large desk piled with stacks of buff folders. The congregation looked as if they'd been waiting forever; as if time were postponed. Their eyes, fixed on the secretary with distilled numbness, shifted to Julia.

'The doctor told me to come.' Julia wondered if the secretary knew. The secretary, a hunchback with a tired face in a tight yellow Lycra t-shirt that hugged her high shoulders, indicated she should sit down. Perhaps she was tired of talking. Perhaps it was forbidden to speak in this tabernacle. Julia chose a front seat and regretted it.

The silent room smelled of burnt toast. Two small girls popped their heads out of a doorway behind the secretary's desk. One, a pretty little thing, came in with a plastic cup and filled it at the water dispenser. Julia stared at the tiled floor. Then at framed hygiene certificates on the wall. A woman with a tiny baby swaddled in a synthetic blue blanket came in. Julia, like the others, watched her.

A door swung shut behind the curtained hallway and a pregnant woman emerged clutching her folder with a confessor's relief. Two women behind Julia followed her out. Was she the only one on her own? She craned her neck to sneak a look at patients and their chaperones. All the women looked like they were expecting. Expecting was a funny way of putting it, thought Julia, who expected little.

Her aunt had said it was better Julia went alone; if you see anyone you know tell them you are having women's problems, they won't ask. Tia Lucila, an English professor at San Carlos, had lived in Chicago nine years, worked out there, put herself through college, married (and divorced) a Gringo. She came home when she couldn't stand another bitter winter. Lucila was the only single woman Julia knew who didn't act like an old-maid; she laughed more than anyone else in her family.

At Lucila's kitchen table, while black beans simmered, Julia tried to put words together. Lucila's hand of magenta nails came to rest on Julia's. Julia watched the clock's minute hand march doggedly, wishing she could turn it back to last week or, better still, a month ago. It made three circuits till Tia spoke.

'I speak to you as though you were my own. We're going to buy something from the chemist to check. If you are, well, folk would say different, but you're too young. It's just an accident. Accidents happen. To me,' she gave Julia's hand a squeeze, 'to everyone. The problem here is the Church. In *Estados Unidos* girls get fixed, no questions asked. Is that what you want?'

Julia nodded, her eyes filling with tears. The thing that happened between her and Juan was so insignificant in the light of its implications. His jeans slipping down his backside, hard hips jerking her thighs against the branches of the coffee tree, the smell of blood and ammonia. The idea somebody was growing inside her filled her with anxiety. A lamb of God, a soul, a precious life; phrases of her priest, her mother and her school teacher – but what had these to do with her, who had barely begun her own?

Julia, top of her class, already had a vague notion she would not follow in her mother's footsteps; married at fifteen, with five living children and two still-born. Every influence whispered motherhood in her ear. Except the one strong example of Tia Lucila; happy, free and single. This anomaly in a culture of families had opened a large space in her heart for Julia, prescient of a different future awaiting her niece. No matter how much Julia adored her younger siblings and her countless cousins, she could not imagine herself into the role of mother.

'Give the beans a stir, *amorcita*, I'll be right back.'

Julia stirred the thickening *frijoles negros*. She stared at the familiar things in Lucila's kitchen like she'd never seen them before: a calendar from the *ferreteria* on Magdalena, a porcelain chick, a plastic Strawberry Shortcake clock. Lucila returned with a small white paper bag. Inside was a packet with a tube inside that she told Julia to pee on. She handed it back to her aunt. They waited in silence. Two blue stripes, like the national flag. Lucila sighed:

'Can you keep it secret? Better if Juan never knows; one word could put us in danger.'

The day dragged. Julia felt hungry but eating made her queasy. Her mother threw her the odd look but was too busy with the baby and the twins to ask. That night she got no sleep.

After school Julia went straight to her aunt's. She sat on her front door step and watched a couple of boys kicking a football around in the plaza. Little girls in pink tutus came prancing out of the ballet school next door. In Julia's barrio kids played in the road. Lucila pulled up in her dusty blue Kia and bustled toward her, arms full of books.

'*Hola, muñeca.*'

Julia followed Lucila up the stairs to the apartment carrying her bag.

'Well I've checked,' Lucila said as she mixed a fresco, 'and we don't have many options. There's one doctor who may help us. I made an appointment for you. Can you manage alone?'

Julia nodded.

And here she was.

The baby at her elbow cried. The mother shifted her huipil and nuzzled it up to her breast. Julia felt a swell of nausea and dashed to the bathroom. Behind the locked door she crouched over the toilet and retched. Wiping tears from her eyes she rinsed her mouth. As she came out, the secretary nodded:

'Go through.'

Through the curtain there were three doors, one was ajar.

121

Behind a Formica desk, below a high window streaming with sunshine, sat a middle-aged man in a polo shirt. He had grey hair and a large birthmark on his left cheek.

'I was wondering...' she faltered.

'Go ahead,' he encouraged.

'I'm pregnant.' She saw his eyelid twitch. 'But I'm not ready to be a mother, since I'm fourteen. My aunt thought you might be able to help.'

'Well, my dear, I can see the problem. But I'm a doctor under oath and it's illegal to terminate in Guate. It's different in Cuba where I'm from.'

A tear slipped down Julia's cheek.

'Are you sure? Here, hop up onto the bed, let me do a scan.'

The doctor pushed the rim of her jeans below her belly-button, rubbed cold jelly on her stomach and passed a squeegee over it. She followed his gaze to the floodlit grainy white cross-section of a ball in a cup that filled the black screen.

'Yes, that's it,' he said. 'About six weeks, I'd say.'

Julia began to sob even as she uncoupled her tenderness from the image of the marine creature in its shell. She could not indulge her emotions; every sentiment must be steeled to one end. The doctor dropped his voice to a whisper:

'There's one thing that you can do...' His voice was so low she had sit up to catch his words.

'But you must promise not to tell anyone I told you. You understand? They sell medicine in la Suiza, opposite Elektra, in the plaza; it's called Cytotec. Have you pen and paper?'

Julia pulled her religion exercise book and Barbie pencil case out of her school bag. She tried to hand the doctor her pencil but he shook his head and spelled it out.

'Four pessaries at the beginning of the night. You need to drink lots and wrap up. There'll be plenty of blood for a couple of weeks. It's risky. Ask your aunt to help. Whatever happens don't mention me.'

Julia stumbled into the waiting room, the reprobate without a buff folder, and out into the bedlam of Coban.

Lucila went straight to the pharmacy. She returned exasperated.

'They won't give us the drug without a prescription.'

'But the doctor won't write one!'

'I know, I've an idea. Don't worry. Come back tomorrow. We'll see if my hunch is right.'

Julia wondered how much more of her life was going to be on hold. Juan had tried to speak to her in the playground that morning but she'd told him she felt sick, to go away.

The next afternoon, at Lucila's kitchen table, her aunt told her there was this guy in Guate, who had once got his girlfriend pregnant and gone through hell to sort it out. He was running an illegal one-man distribution of imported drugs. Lucila had ordered some. She didn't mention they cost half her month's salary.

'You have to persuade your mother to let you stay next weekend. Say I need help with something… hairdressing.'

Saturday morning Lucila drove to País and bought sanitary pads, panties, painkillers and sugary *aguas*. She bought *saldo* for her mobile and filled the tank with gas. She rang a few friends and told them she'd be cutting hair later that day. She sent them home early complaining she had a headache. The sun was setting when Julia took the first dose of Miteprisone. The pills had arrived unlabelled in a white paper envelope; there was no way of knowing what they were. If anything were to happen, the IGGS hospital was eight minutes away; Julia was to say she was having a miscarriage; they had to treat women by law.

Julia watched her aunt undress in the half-light. Her body's sensual solidity was comforting. Julia was glad to be sharing a bed with her. She drifted off quickly but woke with a jerk, in excruciating pain. She cried out before she remembered. Dragging herself onto all fours, she felt a warm rush of blood between her thighs. Lucila was awake, turning on the lamp, her hand on the small of her back.

'It's okay, *amorcita*, it's okay.'

The voice seemed far away. Julia recalled the painting on Coban's municipal wall of Jesus weeping over an aborted foetus, beads of blood splashing down his arms, his badly rendered face contorted by grief. Sin. The sin of sex before marriage. The sin of conceiving out of wedlock. The sin of lying to her mother. The sin of abortion. Things not even whispered at school. She reached for her Tia's hand. Looking into her face she saw a magnificent woman. Despite biting agony she was filled with gratitude and whispered:

'Thank you Tia, thank you.' Sin was not real, she told herself. It was conceived of by men to bring women to heel. She would not be subdued like her mother, sisters or girlfriends. She would be free, like Lucila, whatever the price.

The pain came in waves now and Julia lay on her side. After some time she fell asleep.

The sun was high when she woke. As she lowered her feet to the floor gingerly she felt a void where her stomach once was. Lucila had tortillas, eggs, beans and a pitcher of coffee on the table. She kissed Julia's forehead. They ate in silence. After, as she nursed a sweet mug of coffee, Julia said:

'Tia, when all this is over, I'd like to live with you. I could help you, with the cooking, the hairdressing, whatever.'

Later that morning Lucila drove her to Las Victorias where Coban's lovers cuddled on benches or under trees. They sat by the lake under the sign warning them not to swim because of the crocodile. And in the playground where teenagers played on the wooden frames and swings. They ate *churrasco* near La Cantonal and drank hot chocolate in Acuña's courtyard under the huge avocado tree. Julia let her aunt make a fuss over her before they headed home for the next round of drugs. But nothing more happened, either that night or the next. Lucila wondered if they had the real thing. Maybe the guy in the city was Opus Dei and had sent out slow-working poison. With no excuse for her to stay Julia went home.

Her aunt said they had to wait two weeks before a check-up. Julia's life slowed to a caterpillar pace. Everything dragged. Her friends irritated her with their childishness. Homework was unbearable. Falling asleep, almost impossible. She had that sick feeling *Monja Blancas* gave her on Verapaz roads. Her body started to feel curvy. On the way home from school Juan spoke to her but she couldn't think of anything to say. Before the week was out, word was they weren't *novios* anymore.

When she returned to the doctor's, the waiting room was almost empty and the secretary waved her straight in. She told the doctor she'd had a miscarriage, though she couldn't look him in the eye. He did another scan. This time she screwed her eyes closed.

'Something is still there.'

Julia was too tired to cry; she just stared at him. The doctor sighed:

'There's this specialist I heard about in the city, a German, doing this for twenty years, she's a midwife. I'll give you her number.'

He gave her a paper and pen, spelled out 'SUSANNA' and a phone number.

'She's the only one.'

Julia waited on her aunt's steps with a heavy heart. How many favours could she ask? But she underestimated Lucila; within fifteen minutes she was on the phone to Susanna.

They took the eight-hour bus down to the City with the excuse of Independence Day. A wall of fog bordered the road so that everything appeared magically as they passed and faded the instant after. The rains had wrecked stretches of asphalt and road-workers waving flags kept them waiting as the traffic streamed past in the opposite direction. The sun was setting when they arrived at Octava Avenida. They took a green bus crammed with city-folk to Zona Una. They stayed with an old boyfriend of Lucila's. Everything in his apartment was broken-down and charming. He prepared a delicious *caldo*; Julia had never seen a man cook before. He and Lucila kept up a lively banter all evening; Julia fell asleep on his sofa to their laughter.

In the morning they caught several buses till they reached La Guarda, a market that stretched out over blocks. Police *picops* cruised past busty prostitutes jiggling their hips in fake leather corsets, fishnet stockings and denim minis. Filthy drunks and bug-eyed druggies wove their way between stalls flogging car stereos, wheel hubs, plastic knick knacks and sizzling food. Julia gripped her aunt's hand tightly. They found Quince Avenida, the pink two-storey building with its sign 'Manos Abiertas'.

Inside, a tall foreigner with long grey hair, denim skirt and high heels led Julia to a side-room. Julia lay on a high hospital bed and, covering a plastic tube with jelly and a condom, the doctor gently pushed it inside of her. She frowned at the screen.

'Well, there's nothing alive in there but you still have residual material which needs to come out. What drugs did you take?'

Julia struggled with their names.

'How much?'

'Three hundred of the first and six hundred of the second.'

'That wasn't enough. Where did you get them from?'

'A man in the city...'

'There are a lot of duds knocking around. Well... I can get rid of it now. But I'm afraid it's going to cost.'

'How much?'

'Five hundred *quetzals*.'

Julia went out to the waiting room and whispered to her aunt:

'Five hundred *quetzals*.'

Lucila fished in her handbag for her purse. She counted five crisp hundreds into Julia's hand.

Julia took them to the midwife and followed her into a side room. The secretary shuffled behind a screen, emerging with instruments. The midwife filled a syringe with liquid as Julia sat in a high chair and put her feet into the steel stirrups. The secretary put both her hands firmly on Julia's shoulders. Apologising, the midwife pushed something into her, followed swiftly by the syringe. Julia bit her tongue to stop herself screaming.

'Relax,' said the doctor, rubbing her thigh.

In came other things she couldn't see, each with their own jolt of pain.

'A couple more minutes. You want it all out, don't you?'

'Please,' begged Julia.

When the doctor had finished Julia got down and lay on a bed next door. The secretary went out and came back a minute later with a steaming ginger tea and a hot water bottle. The nurse put it against her stomach.

'Mostly placenta,' said the doctor when she came back. 'All out now. How are you feeling?' Julia nodded. 'I've got another patient... shout if you need anything.'

Julia looked around at the room. Her eyes came to rest on the minute hand scurrying around the clock's face and a huge wave of relief washed over her. What had happened belonged to the past. The yellow walls and soft light filtering through the curtain calmed her. She reached down, pulled the fleece over her shoulders and shut her eyes.

There would be no more waiting. Life would move forward. Julia would move in with her aunt. She would study business at Coban University. She would never marry, though she'd have two more lovers. She would be one of the few women to win a place in Congress. And become the first advocate of sex education in secondary schools. And she would try to make contraception freely available at Centros de Salud. But she didn't get far with that idea.

At the age of thirty-three, somewhat overshadowed by the Otto Perez Molina debacle, she would be the three hundred and second woman (of nine hundred and fifty-nine) to be murdered that year.

The Black Christ's Modest Miracle

Uno

I've hung on this cross for four hundred and thirteen years, six months and nine days. Two hundred and seventy in this Basilica and a hundred and forty-three in the church in Santiago, a mile from here. Not counting the year it took six Chorti villagers to bring Me from La Antigua, capital of the Vice-royalty, stretching from Chiapas to Panama. Man is predictably inconsistent. Having lost lives defending themselves against Conquistadors and the Word, the Chorti sent a delegate to the Bishop to commission Me and set themselves toiling to pay the sculptor, Cataño, for his masterpiece carved from dark balsam wood: the Black Christ. An envoy walked several months to fetch Me; an epic journey laced with unexpected hospitality, bizarre fruits and strange languages. The villagers discovered how diverse their motherland was, before outsiders tried, and failed, to inflict hegemony upon it.

*

My husband Milo and I were the first to arrive beneath the municipal arches. Ladinos claim we're late for everything; yet without a clock we rise before dawn and finish our labours at dusk. Milo has milked Mariposa and Manchitas by first light. He cycles along adoquin streets, basket full of two-litre Pepsi bottles brimming with warm milk. '*Leche! Leche!*' A raft of imitators echoes him: '*Leche! Leche!*' He's so deaf women have to throw their shoe in front of his wheel to stop him or he sails past. Then he leads his cows to pasture and tends to our maize and coffee. He eats and siestas under a *jocote* tree, returning home when the sun falls behind the hills. Meanwhile I wash, boil and husk maize, carry it to mill, mix it with lime and water and prepare *tortillas* with my daughters. We sweep the dirt yard, clean house and scrub clothes.

But tonight is special: Milo, my boy Tonish and I are making a pilgrimage to Esquipulas.

'Don't fret, Mami Celeste,' the girls said. 'We'll take care of things!'

My eldest son, back from El Salvador, will attend to Milo's tasks. My boy Tonish is the head chorister and he arranged the trip. I'm going for one reason; to pray for his soul.

*

Hugo and I showed up after midnight: we'd downed a couple of beers and snatched a moment alone. Mami Celeste and Papi Milo were already there. Women waited in scattered groups under the municipal arches: old ladies squatting; fat ones leaning against pillars; giggling girls in *faldas*. Rain fell, stopped and started again, lightning flashed soundlessly. Cousin Saul, our dopey *chofer*, showed up, and Hugo called out thirty-one names. They took their places, women cramming full baskets overhead and wide hips into seats. We said the Padre Nuestro and Jorge, the dwarf priest, gave his blessings. Hugo set off a string of fireworks and we spluttered off into cobalt night, his thigh against mine.

Dos

The Chorti had the misfortune to live in the shadow of an extinct volcano, Quetzaltepeque, a fertile Eden. When gawky, fair Castilians set eyes on the wending Montagua river, bordered with camel-hump hills, they fixed their grasping hearts on it. Their Promised Land was peopled by principled, unarmed heathens. The Chorti tilled maize; pressed, boiled and set cane into sugar blocks; rode horses and mules. In their virtuous, full lives there was no room for suspicion. When the Castilians shifted from abuse of hospitality to outright occupation the Chorti defended their valley for three blood-drenched days and nights.

The Spaniards were ready to kill every last one so the Chorti gave in. Having robbed them of Utopia, the Conquistadors rewarded them with Old Testament aphorisms about camels and eyes of needles. The Chorti had never seen a camel.

*

Saul, my nephew and godchild, is our driver. I saw him baptised, married and his daughters christened and confirmed. A good-hearted, broad fellow, without a tooth in his jaw, who saved up and drove to New Mexico to buy this school bus. A handsome Blue Bird it is too: not a scratch on the yellow paint, gleaming chrome and vinyl letters on the windscreen with his girls' names: 'Lucy and Linda'. Above the mirror, the eagle and the Yanqui flag, lit with blue neon, flash on off, on off all night. My boy, Tonish, has no kids, no wife, not even a sweetheart. Milo gave up taking him to the fields years ago, says he's less use than his sisters. Tonish is a good lad; stays close to home and helps us. He's a clever boy, but there's not much for *güiros* to do in our village of farmers and coffin-makers: Tonish lives for the choir and Hugo.

We expect our boys to marry, work and worship in the same church. I don't let the sneers on neighbours' faces bother me. Christ never married. He spent his life with men; once with a whore even. My other son has a wife, three kids: they grew up in the same house; same school; same church: same sisters. One loves girls, the other...

*

North of the city we got stuck at road works for two hours. Nobody complained; it's not their way. Dawn was divine: sublime rays slipping across mountains overflowing with waterfalls and greenery. If you believe in God, you'd think He'd arranged it on purpose. I do, but not like the others. Their God is a grouchy old bastard with a maudlin wimp of a son. Mine is earthy: he sweats, laughs and wanks like us. If I bumped into Jesus I'd give him a taste of my Elysian Fields.

Further along, a bus was parked on the verge, displaced passengers staring off into space. As we slowed to pass, we saw a corpse under a white sheet. Poor *cerote*, never made it to Esquipulas: bugger lacked faith, I s'pose.

Tres

They collected Me from the workshop at the end of rainy season on Saint Francis' Day: a mute, glassy-eyed crew overwhelmed by La Antigua's elegant churches, residences and cobbled streets. None had seen such brilliant workmanship as Cataño's, blurring boundaries between craft, art and divinity. Smitten, they mumbled amongst themselves over how to bring Me home. Cataño had one of his boys hammer together a float with crossbars like those used for Semana Santa.

At each village en route, folk begged them to stay to pay homage. It took them the better part of a year to get Me to Esquipulas. When they arrived, the Chorti had built Me a simple maize-cane hut. It served at first, but it wasn't long before word spread, drawing crowds from further afield: a proper church was called for.

*

We spent the morning shopping. At the foot of the Basilica lies a maze of stalls selling mementos and sweets. Tonish wanted to buy a Day-Glo Virgin Mary that shifts into a luminous Christ as you walk past, but he hadn't enough *quetzalitos*. The kids begged for straw hats decorated with ribbon, tinsel and baskets. We pitched in for garlands to dress the bus. Tonish tied the stencilled sign to the bumper and read the words out loud: 'San Antonio's Church Choir Silver Anniversary Celebration'.

*

Shuffling into the church we made a circle around the Black Christ. Not at all like the usual skinny, miserable yellow plaster ones you see with *pitaya*-pink blood, flared nostrils and dead eyes. This one writhed on the cross: high cheekbones, long curls, open arms, nicely toned muscles. Everything about Him was consummate. What a cute contrast His taut limbs would make beneath my fleshiness. I can picture what's under His loincloth perfectly: sweeter than *zapote*, smoother than avocado, rigid as yucca root. The kind of man I wouldn't kick out of bed. Absolute devotion? You bet.

Cuatro

Faith accounts for everything. Kant thought he'd invented the theory of perception but the Church understood it long before. The first pilgrim whose conviction was greater than his ego was a Mexican aristocrat who cured himself of a terminal illness. Didn't take long for that to reach the ears of every hypochondriac in the Americas. Month after month they came: barefoot labourers feverish with dengue jostling with moustached landowners yanking unwed, gourd-bellied daughters. The candle light barely pierced the resin's smog that burnished My complexion. I tanned to the hue of cocoa beans, like the Mayans who worshipped Me. Rumours of a miracle began to circulate.

A hundred years later, the Peruvian Archbishop of Guatemala made the journey, curing himself of homesickness. Over the next two hundred years thousands came: riddled with smallpox, gangrene or syphilis. Their wanting tires Me. Innumerable candles drip stalactites, slipping and sliding, puddling the tiles with annatto reds, cochineal blues, saffron yellows and pine greens.

*

In the muddy lot filled with buses, we unwrapped our parcels and breakfasted on leftovers, washed down with Pepsi. The Basilica, white as confirmation satin, gleamed against the green hills, the gold dome dazzling as a crown. There were many pilgrims, though few wore traditional dress like us. We drew curious stares as we made our way through the *mercado* to the pleasant gardens filled with tall *llama de bosque*, dropping waxy orange blossoms. A torch burned brightly in a side-chapel.

Inside, the walls were plastered with silver votives, hammered into legs, hearts, babies or eyes. I wished I had one, to avoid shaping my petition in words – but they haven't fashioned one for mine yet. We waited in line, shuffling slowly toward the Black Jesus. Weeping parents, at His feet, sobbing over lost children moved me. Pain filled my chest. Under the staggering weight of their sorrow I forgot the entreaty I'd come to make. As we took our leave, stumbling backwards, I had a realisation about my boy Tonish: he may not be what I'd hoped for but he's alive and kicking.

*

They took photos of each other in front of the Basilica holding the choir's blue and white banner: Mama Celeste and Papa Milo, Great Aunt Irla, the cousins Joni and Merli, Nicey and Jeferson holding hands. The girls patted their hair smooth, the boys puffed out their chests. The runners changed into their tennis and t-shirts, lit Independence Day torches and set off. Everyone cheered when the bus caught up. We stopped at Pasa Buena around lunchtime. Hugo and I went to 'stretch our legs'. He was sulky but that didn't put me off: I like him moody, adds a bit of edge. Returning in good spirits I devoured a lunch of leftovers. Then we rolled up our trousers and waded in the chill river. And lay in the shade of the pine trees while the kids splashed.

Just before we set off for the long drive home, through holiday traffic, Mama Celeste grabbed my hand. She brushed her palm across my cheek the way she used to when I was a kid, eyes wet with tears, murmuring something about a tiny miracle.

The Pineapple Seller

Berta wakes on Sunday morning with the worst headache she's ever had. She keeps her eyes shut at first. It comes back to her in a series of pictures, like ads on the highway. Of Chepe's silhouette, leant against the door frame, reeking of *aguardiente*. Of his arm raised and Jenifer crying out. Of the crack on her brow and thinking 'fall back, fall back' so as not to hurt the baby. But it woke the baby up. And if the cries of the girls weren't enough, and the yard dogs howling, the screaming baby did it. 'He's at it again,' she could almost hear her neighbours grumbling, shaking their heads.

She lifts her hand to her brow and cries out when she feels the bump: there'll be no hiding it. She opens her eyes but the bruised one is sealed shut. Through the other she sees first light, seeping below the shutter onto the sill. She raises herself on her elbow. The girls are curled up in bed – Luisa, her arm protectively about Jenifer, the baby near the foot. Chepe's nowhere to be seen. Berta gets up, stiffly, and hobbles to the tin door and into the yard. On the other side, past the room where her sister and parents sleep, there are the latrine and shower – three breeze block walls open to the yard. From the high opening behind the shower head, she pulls down a small, round plastic-framed mirror and examines the eye. It's the colour of plums, grainy like *moco* skin, the size of a strawberry. What she would give to have some of that powder Ladino women dust their cheeks with.

She takes a cold shower and puts the same dress and apron back on. Her mother's awake, at the *pila*, washing last night's dishes. She nods good morning as Berta fills her bucket with water but doesn't notice the black eye. Her mother's seen so much in her long life, she doesn't want to see more. Berta wakes her daughters, brushes and plaits their hair and gives them a cold tortilla to share. She ties the baby into her *morral* and they leave. Berta lugs a sloshing bucket, Luisa carries an empty one and holds Jenifer's hand. They hurry silently down the dirt path to the main plaza. Miguel's in front of the church, revving impatiently. Acuarina's already there. Brenda comes scurrying, with her four. They clamber onto the pick-up and they're off, dust cloud trailing. No one mentions Berta's bruise. On the road, they pack their baskets to the brim with pineapples from the mountain, loose on the pick-up floor. Miguel picks up another two women at the roadside and drops Brenda off.

Berta's next. Miguel hauls her basket onto the bank for her. She follows, with buckets and children, waving goodbye to the disappearing pick-up. She unpacks her things: chopping board, plastic bags, knife. Sprinkling a handful of water over the table, she washes it down with her palm and sets to work. Her blade severs pineapple crowns and studded armour in seconds. Quartering each with a few deft chops, she scoops the triangles into bags and hangs them on nails above her head.

When the baby wakes she opens the buttons of her flowered dress and lets it feed. The girls play with the leaf-cutting ants in the grass behind the stall, giggling softly: Jenifer's is a cane truck, Luisa's a police car. The cane truck takes the lead. Luisa, squealing with frustration, squashes it with the heel of her hand before it crosses the stick that marks the finishing line. Jenifer wrestles her down into the grass. Berta looks down the road to where it peters away at the bend.

Soon this stretch, between Siquinalá and Santa Lucía Cotzumalguapa, will be bumper to bumper. First just the odd pick-up of labourers or a Bluebird heading towards Mazatenango or Retalhuleu. Then motorcycles, tuc-tucs, cars and cane-sugar trucks huffing billows of black smoke into the air. The roads are overburdened: every day the traffic increases. The trucks come from Mexico or the States and south from countries Berta's never heard of. Too many cars means customers won't pull over to buy her three-*quetzal* bags of pineapple. Progress implies other bad things too. In the city they sell pineapple in tins: there are machines that do her job, faster. They dry pineapple pieces too.

Her first customer is a whale of a man driving a long Chiquita banana truck.

'If you knew how badly I need pineapple: I dreamt about it. My wife says I'm crazy – bananas in the back and all I think of is pineapple.' She smiles.

'How much further to Escuintla?' he mumbles, juice dripping down his chin.

'Six miles – but that way,' pointing in the direction he came from.

'Púchica! How did I miss it?' She shrugs. He's already on his third triangle by the time he swings himself into his cabin.

'If only I could be with a man like that,' thinks Berta, 'fat and happy.'

She throws her knife down, hand on hip, and watches him make an impossible U-turn, backing up into a dirt road. He drives past and gives her a wave. Two minutes later she's forgotten him.

Camilo settles himself behind the wheel. The cabs are spacious, built for big men in countries where men are bigger, but Camilo is huge. Fat in the dramatic way Ladinos often are. His artless features (snub nose, gentle eyes and child's mouth) are the only parts, besides his hands and penis, which have kept their original shape. Tufty curls and steel-rimmed glasses add to his ingenuous appearance. From the chin down, each fold of fat is stacked on a larger ledge, until somewhere below the hips he begins to narrow. Always burly, he was never going to end up in the fields. His uncle taught him to drive and he delivered *champurradas* to Tiquizate's shops till he was old enough to get his class A.

In the old job he'd head to the sub-contractor on a Monday

morning and wait for an assignment. Sometimes he'd wait a day, sometimes two. Then he'd get a three-day job that might take seven, what with borders and waiting at the port. He'd earn six hundred *quetzals*. Total. On the road, he spent forty a day on food, five for a shower. Sleeping in the truck and petrol fumes were free. He's driven a *flota dedicada* since he was twenty-four, hauling sugar, coffee or fertiliser. Things with Chiquita will be better: shifts are twenty-four hours, twenty-five days a month. He picked up his first forty-three foot container this morning at Neuva Concepción. The supervisor gave him enough money for the chiller and fuel to Puerto Barrios. He said it'll take Camilo around nine hours there and six back – but he's never left the depot.

When he signed his contract, the boss gave him a pamphlet with a cartoon of Miss Chiquita, her slinky arm around a worker. He couldn't read it, but Alvaro, his brother-in-law, told him it said he had rights. Alvaro was an accountant for a Jewish family in Retalhuleu. Camilo had asked:

'What sort of rights?'

'It says that alongside making money and growing quality bananas Chiquita have good relationships with their workers. Says they value integrity and responsibility. Says they want to hear your opinions, they respect international law, you're allowed to gather freely to discuss your conditions, you shouldn't work more than forty-eight hours a week, the company will always tell the truth, blah, blah, blah. It's bullshit, of course; they're Chiquita.'

'And?'

'The United Fruit Company under another name.'

'So?'

'You're too young to remember.' Alvaro was only five years older.

'There are five companies who control the banana market. They used to own the land, but they found it was cheaper not to, so they set one grower against the other. American supermarkets take forty per cent of the profits, the growers, two.'

Camilo remembered his job interview, his finger tied to a lie detector. He'd answered questions like 'Are you a paedophile?' and 'Are you part of a union?'

'What can I do? I need work.'

'Of course, just don't trust them.'

This morning he woke up dizzy with a thirst he can't shake. He's tired and irritable. His vision is blurring – probably why he missed the turn to Escuintla. He's hungry and needs to pee. He didn't tell the pineapple seller it's his third pineapple that morning.

Even before the business with the union, Camilo told his best friend, Pio, not to get involved. Pio joined the *sindicato* on the sly and their boss stung him with a *carta negra*: he'd never work again. Not as a driver. What else could he do after seventeen years? Camilo's solidarity was enough to get him the sack. It seemed like he'd never find a new job. Off work three months, his wife lost the baby. When their nine-year old girl got fever they couldn't take her to hospital. Paulito should have been bringing in a wage but he'd fallen in with a bad crowd. The smaller three were barely under control.

His wife knows something is wrong with Camilo, but she doesn't ask. Things haven't been the same lately. Instead of playing with the kids he doles out blows like candy. Selling tortillas in the shade of the cathedral doesn't keep body and soul together: she's glad of his job with Chiquita, it's easier when he's away.

The road is strewn with bits of cane, fallen from trucks. He thinks of the girls at the port. The other truckers fuck them. Not him. They cry on his shoulder and share their secrets. He thinks of the Gallo he'll drink, cold and bitter. The eggs, black beans, fried plantain and sour cream. And a few hours' sleep. As he swallows sweet-sour pineapple, he feels the sugar in his veins, but it's not enough. After the girls, the Gallo, dinner and a good night's sleep is the long drive home again. Back to his wife complaining about noisy Evangelicals, of dust that coats everything and the chickenfeed they survive on. He feels palpitations and grabs another triangle of pineapple.

The radio receives better than in his old truck. He fiddles with the knob till he gets a Mexican station, the news:

'Banana company Chiquita Brands International said on Wednesday it has agreed to a $25 million fine and admits paying a Colombian terrorist group for protection in a volatile part of the country. This is just the latest of many scandals that the company, once known as United Fruit, has been involved in. A 1928 strike at its Colombia operations was quelled by army troops who opened fire, killing 1,000 of its own workers. In 1954, the company helped foment the coup against Guatemalan President Jacob Arbenz which threw the country into thirty years of civil war.'

Camilo's eyesight blurs as he feels invisible tentacles grip his chest and squeeze.

'Earlier this decade, Human Rights Watch linked Chiquita with companies that used child labour in Ecuador. In court documents filed Wednesday, federal prosecutors said the Cincinnati-based company and several unnamed high-ranking corporate officers paid around $1.7 million between 1997 and 2004...'

He gasps for air, but there's none to be had.

'... to the AUC which has been responsible for some of the worst massacres in Colombia's civil conflict and for a sizeable percentage of the country's cocaine exports. The right-wing group was designated by the U.S. government as a terrorist organisation...'

He presses his foot on the brakes and fumbles for the handbrake. Darkness closes in.

*

'Mama, why are there so many ants?' Jenifer asks Berta.

'God makes as many as He needs,' answers Berta shortly.

She wonders what's causing the slow-down so early. Drivers sit patiently at first. One or two get out and disappear around the corner to have a look. A scrawny fellow buys a bag of pineapple slices. His wife wants one, then his kids. A cane trucker hops down and buys some. Some labourers on a pick-up jump down, too. Further back, a lady on a bus calls out for a bag. Berta sends Jenifer over. Then everyone wants one. The girls run to and fro with bags of pineapple, bringing the grubby notes and the coins back to Berta. Her ready stock is demolished in a few minutes. She sets to work trimming as fast as she can. She gets Luisa, on the upside-down bucket, to put the slices in the bags and Jenifer to ferry them to customers.

One by one the passengers give in to the sweet-sour fruit, relief from the sun's heat, so much stronger when they're stationary. A few cars overtake on the left lane, seeing it empty. Soon they're double-parked in front of the pineapple seller. The police pick-up arrives, squeezing along the remaining strip of tarmac. A policeman jumps down and buys six bags of pineapple. An ambulance shows up.

By the time the traffic starts to move, Berta has sold every last pineapple. When Miguel returns, freed from the snarl, he promises to bring her more:

'Today's our lucky day, Berta! Sold more today than you do in a week.'

On their way back, the police are disappointed she's sold out. A Chiquita banana truck, they tell her, jack-knifed right in the middle of the road. A heart attack, they say. And laugh, not unkindly: he was such a fat guy it took four men to squeeze him out of the cab.

Gorin

'*Es mi hermana!*' Sister, my sister. She cries over and over, hands locked around her sister's throat.

To start with that's all Ula understands. Will nobody stop them? It's not her business. Yet…

The agency mothers gape. They're visiting San Antonio Aguas Calientes' craft market for an afternoon's shopping. They've not known each other long but, far from home and longer in Guatemala than any had planned, they made friends fast. The shifting bureaucracy that kept Mayans in their place for centuries tyrannises everyone today. 'Foreign cultures cannot be explained by common sense,' Ula habitually advised her high-paying clients. 'You have to work with, not against, them.' She reminds herself of this nugget of vicarious wisdom now she needs it herself.

But sense, common or otherwise, does not apply to Guatemala's labyrinthine adoption process. For six months Ula has been to and from the capital, trying not to breathe choking fumes or dwell on its sprawling ugliness and millions of scuttling residents. She's been in and out of dusty government offices waiting for civil servants, seething with unspecified resentment, to sign documents. Back and forth to immutable lawyers with stiff necks and piles of jaundiced folders, crammed with pages of dot-matrix text plastered with stamps. And always little Gorin in her front pack, bursting with bottles of formula, disposable diapers, scented wipes and toys. But no matter how hot or tearful Ula gets, Gorin remains calm.

She's lucky, she reminds herself. Unlike most of the agency mothers, she has decent Spanish. And her husband visits every couple of months. She's blessed with a mother who helps. And the biggest break of all; Gorin's perfect. But, as they say at the agency, you get the child you deserve. With his pelt of jet hair and olive skin, he's a charmer. Little Gorin's the finishing touch on a career settling corporate ex-pats and a marriage to a publishing house heir.

Her only concern is Gorin's sublime indifference. Signild noticed at once. So typical of her mother, a few hours off the plane from Stockholm, to pick up on the significant detail, establishing her superiority. Ula hasn't mentioned it to the agency mothers who opine indigenous babies are inherently placid, whether nurture or nature is responsible they can only guess. Nonetheless she made a discreet appointment with an eye specialist in Guatemala City. He did the slit lamp test, the swinging flash light exam and placed a headset on little Gorin. He mumbled something about poor pupil reactions: the lottery of adoption, malnutrition and Leber's Congenital Amaurosis. DNA tests were sent off and would be back within a week. In the interim, Signild's nagging presence was Ula's major preoccupation. Ula found herself organising time with the agency mothers.

'How quickly we women adapt,' she remarked to the post-feminist women, 'from being single to motherhood, from having careers to being carers.' They smiled, unsure if she was complimenting or indicting them. Adaptation was, after all, the key to both survival and extinction.

Ula was in good shape for a woman her age. But the caveat undermined the statement. She'd been passably pretty: blond hair, blue eyes, a good figure, the details hadn't mattered. A blousey ripeness that flamed and withered quickly. Now when she studied her reflection, all she saw was encroaching age: lumpiness where curves had been, cheeks marred by crows' feet. Like a page of scrawls; an arbitrary lottery of doodles and crossings-out. Youth had been delightfully unpredictable, but contradictions set in. And all the while, Signild loomed large like some matriarchal archetype of a Norse myth, the spirit of venerable serenity. Preserved in a wintry spring, she was unwaveringly triumphant in her determination to grow old with dignity.

By her own account, Signild had given birth at forty-five, before the days of amniocentesis, labour barely interrupting lunch. She returned to her job as a social worker in six weeks yet breast-fed till Ula could chew. Ula, perversely, had hurtled towards middle age and was past childbearing at forty. Her body, once weightless and resilient, defied her: she understood it through its deficiencies. Unpredictable periods intensified, emotions atrophied into symptoms. Other men's gaze rested on her less and fewer gentlemanly gestures were made, now she sought them. Her long-suffering husband stood by, loyal and resentful to the last. Gorin was just what they needed.

La Antigua wasn't such a bad place to spend a year. Picturesque enough to fill a brochure several times over, surrounded by three volcanoes, quake ruins undisturbed for two centuries, neglect preserving its colonial beauty until UNESCO took it under its wing. Restoration, with the affluent Ladino and visitor in mind, had smoothed the town's rough edges. Too much polishing had burnished it to a fake lustre. Classy restaurants, hotels and discreet beauty salons glistened in its cobbled streets. Even by Minnesota's standards it was slick. This wasn't the real Guatemala if that was what you were after. Ula was sure she wasn't – but she didn't want her husband, arrived yesterday, to think adopting had dulled her sense of adventure.

But having Gorin had changed her. She hadn't suffered childbirth, or the haze of suckling, but she was as tied to this child as much as any mother. Serene Buddha though he was, he demanded attention. His nappies and hunger, forethought. While she adjusted from executive to domestic, Alex was exploring the single life, second time around. No matter how mutual their considered decision was, she was on this leg of parenting alone. Of course he wanted to be there, but someone had to pay the agency's and lawyers' fees. She reassured herself that this was just a fleeting interlude; soon she'd be back in Minneapolis's rat race, sending Gorin off to nursery, firing orders at home help as she gulped down her muesli.

So, she'd invited the agency mothers for a lunch and an outing. Signild was the perfect hostess, of course, making Kottbüllar and Janssöns Frestelse to go with the Akvavit. What she had lacked as a mother, Signild made up for as a grandmother, baffling Ula. Alex was in top form, separation had done him good; he was as attentive toward her as when they first met. As the guests showed up he introduced himself, managing to ask after a detail or two of their lives, proving he'd been listening to her on those long-distance calls.

There was Bessie, the stockbroker, whose husband sent a steady flow of exotic flowers and Swiss chocolates from Wall Street. And Estelle, the blond New York liver specialist, adopting her second. The jolly Helena, a criminal lawyer. And Lisbeth, the psychoanalyst and Andrea, the design consultant. All top-notch, professional women who'd got to a certain age and found it was too late. Some, taking note of mothers' stress and grandmothers' joy, had intentionally bypassed the prescribed biological window to the gateway to the golden years. Having spent fertile decades avoiding impregnation, the latter ones had been engaged inducing it. Failing, they'd opted to rescue a child from an underdeveloped country.

But the defensive note that had crept into Ula's voice had not escaped Alex.

'If you saw the conditions these kids are raised in,' she told him on those late-night calls, 'you'd die, they're hovels with dirt floors and corrugated roofs. Running from one car to the next at traffic lights, selling Kleenex or phone cards. Mothers, unable to feed a first, have another and another. Fathers, passed out cold in the street, start new families before the first has been weaned.'

Not so different from our ghettos, thought Alex, but he was

new man enough not to contradict her.

'I want to come home,' she cried. They made her feel queasy; the fat women with gold teeth and plaits who never stopped smiling, the men with sullen, closed faces. They only spoke to Ula to sell things. They were too many, indistinct and dangerous.

'You always have to watch your wallet, hide your camera, not wear jewellery,' she told Alex. As she'd been told. Guatemala had recorded six thousand murders last year, many were victims of domestic violence. Hardly the sort a baby should be exposed to.

'Take Gorin's birth mother,' (that's what they call them at the agency) 'this unmarried girl, practically a child, pretended Eber,' (as Gorin was christened) 'was her sister's, to avoid church censure. But, unable to feed him, she gave him up.'

The agency offered Ula the chance to meet Eber's aunt, but she chose not to. She hadn't admitted, even to herself, the reason. Supposing the birth mother wanted Eber back when she saw Gorin. Having never had one of her own (abortions didn't count) she could only guess at that umbilical bond Signild gushed about. And never mind the birth mother, suppose Gorin betrayed some special affection toward her. It would break Ula's heart. For this reason, lawyers were paid, intermediaries' palms greased and endless papers signed and stamped. So that Ula, not the birth mother, was recognised as Gorin's one and only.

The luncheon had gone well. The women chatted as they cradled dark-eyed babies. Toddlers gurgled and splashed in the fountain. A creepy Texan guy, whose wife was sick, brought his precocious foster-child and had inappropriate conversations with girls old enough to listen. They polished off two bottles of Akvavit, all of Signild's delicacies and bellowed out a traditional Swedish drinking ditty. Then they clambered into the hired minibus for San Antonio Aguas Calientes and bounced along a pot-holed road to the highway that curled up a mountain and down into a mess of grey breeze-block and rusty roofs. The driver pulled up to the artisans' market and slid back the doors.

The plaza was charming, with its stone fountain and bare whitewashed church filled with candles and flowers. The municipal building was decked with orange balloons and huge tarps printed with photos of a presidential candidate: a greying ex-general, fist raised. Men in orange t-shirts were inflating huge paper balloons with electric fans. They filled them with hot air till, billowing, they let them go. Kids watched them drift toward the mountains till they lost colour and eventually form. Alex headed into the square, undoing his camera case as he went.

The agency mothers unfolded three-wheel prams or slung on front-packs and hesitated on the steps between the brilliant sunshine and the market gloom. Inside, weavers knelt on the floor, looms belted to their waists at one end and to pillars at the other. The mothers dispersed in twos and threes, filling the expanse with enthusiasm over wares that covered every conceivable inch of wall. Ula felt unease ricochet around the room as the weavers registered the contradiction between the babies' Mayan features and the mothers' Caucasian ones. She hung back.

'What a pretty girl you are. With curls too! How old?' she asked a child sitting on the steps, playing with a stuffed doll.

'Five,' a fine-featured mother, in the first stall, answered.

'What's your name, *nena*?'

'Monica,' her mother cut in, wavering between resentment and the chance of a sale.

'This is Gorin.'

'From where?'

'I don't know exactly... the orphanage – Hermano Pedro.'

A small group of weavers gathered around Ula cooing and calling to Gorin in terse Cakchiquel. One, a particularly slight woman, bent to kiss his forehead. Ula had heard of child-kidnappers lynched in Kiché and of babies snatched from mother's arms as they waited for a bus or pick-up. She gave a nervous smile and tried to push on, but weavers surrounded her. Flustered, she gripped Gorin tightly and he began to cry. She pulled free of the circle and made for the doorway. She sank down on the steps, heart hammering.

Signild sat down beside her, clutching a garish bedspread destined to look out of place in the ashen tones of her Stockholm apartment. Ula breathed deeply and focused on the square before her; the statue of a woman pouring water, communal *pila*, *figus* and tamarind trees. She'd lived here six months and understood so little.

Just as she's recovering, Monica's fine-boned mother walks briskly toward her, arm in arm with a young girl. The girl is dressed in traje, her skin is patchy and her dark eyes stare, unwavering, beyond the village into the mountains. Everything slows for Ula. They stop a few inches in front of her. Monica's mother guides the girl's hand to Gorin's face. She traces his profile with her fingers and runs them through his thick hair. Her expression of disbelief transforms into one of horror. Ula braces herself. The girl says nothing and pushes past her. Signild smooths the bedspread on her lap:

'I knew you wouldn't like it, but I wanted a bit of Guatemala to remind me of my stay.'

Alex, sitting between them, is editing his photos.

'No, no,' he protests half-heartedly, 'it'll add warmth to your place.'

Church bells peal, crashing and reverberating. As they die, a brass band starts a funeral march drawing the Gringas onto the street to watch. Women sway single file on the left, men to the right, silver and bronze coffin swinging on their shoulders.

All at once, from inside the market, comes a terrible commotion: shuffling, slapping and shrieking. Ula turns to see the blind girl dragging another by her hair. By the time they're in the street, the elder's plait is undone, her *huipil* loose; she's whimpering, head tucked under like a roosting bird. By now, everyone is watching.

'For goodness sake, somebody stop them!' cries Lisbeth.

'How awful!' screams Bessie.

But they all stand as still as the statue of the water carrier.

'*Mi hermana. Es mi hermana.*' Sister, my sister.

Ula hears the blind girl's anguish before she understands the words. Accusation or justification, she can't make out which at first: the girl is hysterical. Ula puts it together.

'You said he was dead. How could you lie to me, *hermana*? You told me he was swept away by the river. I believed you... is that the way to treat your own sister? While I was grinding maize to bring in a few *quetzalitos*, you sold your own flesh and blood to strangers, like he was a basket of *tortillas*. That's where the money came from for the stove and the *lamina* roof. *Mi hermana!*'

'He was going blind... *Ala gran*! We couldn't keep another.'

Ula lets go of her front pack to seal her palms over her ears as a low moan comes from her own mouth. Upset by his birth mother's screaming or Ula's wail, Gorin, or Eber, begins to cry. The driver grabs Ula's arm and bundles her into the minibus, shooing the others after.

The blind girl lifts her face at the slam of the sliding door. The driver starts the engine. As he shifts into first she comes toward them, cheeks stained with tears and eyelids swollen. She scratches at the glass:

'*Mi hijo, mi hijo, mi hijo.*' My son, my son, my son.

The driver steps on the gas and accelerates out of the square.

Ula's breath mists the window as she stares out at the village.

For the first time since she's arrived she sees clearly. The cracks in adobe walls over which bougainvillea blossom spills. The gloss on a lime tree's leaves. Children laughing as they chase a chicken. An old man, dwarfed by a bundle of cilantro, climbs a rocky path in Wellingtons. A farmer's machete swings from his belt as he overtakes the bus on his cycle. Beyond, lie *milpas* dividing absurdly steep, green mountains into handkerchiefs of land.

Story-book clouds mingle with smoke, rising from the volcano.

Things Gorin will never see. For a single moment, one that will never ever be repeated, she feels doubt.

She looks down at this baby, staring contentedly into space. At least in America no one will sell him, she tells herself. At least he'll learn to read Braille and go to a special school. At least…

Green Peaches

The day after La Raña was kidnapped, a truck stacked with furniture ground to a halt on the dirt road. A stocky man, a tiny woman carrying a baby and a plump girl got out with the driver and boys.

'The Castillo family,' the ugly Doña, with patchy brown skin, announced to us. Mamacita said nothing, just stared, arms folded over her belly. Their boys unloaded their things into La Raña's weekend house across the road.

News had come that morning of the bodies, found on the roadside, arms butchered into chunks like *churrasco*. The day before, Tio Bernardo saw eight gunmen push La Raña and the *diputado* into a black pick-up and drive off. That Sunday, Kansas Joe delivered a sermon on the seventh commandment; stealing people is punishable by death. Kansas Joe said God set the commandments in stone for good reason. Mynor whispered there was no paper in Moses' lifetime so He'd had no choice.

La Raña's son dropped in on the Castillos, a pistol tucked into the back of his jeans, later that day. Months passed but no-one got caught, which makes me wonder about God. What's the point of engraving commandments if you're not going to follow up? P'raps He's distracted or, like Mamacita, He's nuts (that's what they say about her around here). Mamacita turned the whole thing into el Señor's hands. She's short on words with most, but she speaks plenty with Him… but she takes a different tone to Kansas Joe.

When I peered through the gate Doña Castillo was yapping orders at the maid. A little girl with sad brown eyes was sitting on the steps, thumb in her mouth, stroking her dog. I asked if she could play: the Doña said we mustn't go far. I showed her the River Chi'o, our house, Papi's cows, our dog Mika and the mill. Belen's only six, though she acts big. But I'm prettier; my cheeks are full as ripe melons, my hair the colour of toasted maize and my eyes black as *zapote* stones. And the wickedest – my nickname's la Llorona.

Belen only has one baby brother. We are eight. Two pick tea at Chirripeco, the eldest works in the City; only Mama, me, Mynor, Paco and the baby, Chiquillo, remain. Nine if you count Papi; even though he left after Chiquillo was born, he still counts around here. There are three families in the Barrio; ours, Papi's new one and Tio Estuardo's. Thirty or so siblings, half-siblings and cousins populate our bumpy road. We've hollow cheeks, fair hair and hungry eyes the colour of the river in rainy season. We call folk on the other side of the river 'shadows'; dark and skinny, you only see them at dawn or dusk.

The first and only time we were invited to Belen's, Mynor asked to borrow books but the Doña said no. So he sneaked out a couple under his t-shirt. We weren't invited again. Their maid throws stones at Mika and shouts at us. But last weekend, Doña Castillo stopped me in the street and asked if I'd feed their dog, Rudi, while they were away. She gave me three tuppers full of meat, bones and rice. I ate the livers myself and fed the rice to Mika. Still, his ribs stick through his fur like the struts of a loom, not like Rudi, plump and as silky as a corncob's beard.

On Saturday, while Mamacita was dozing, I slipped out. Mynor followed.

'Where are you sneaking off to?'

'To feed Rudi.'

'With what?'

He scrambled after me, through the plot of weeds, over the fence and into the Castillos' garden.

'If you're going to be a pain, go home.'

I hoisted myself up to the star-shaped open window to Belen's room and squinted in. I could make out the desk in the darkness. When my arms ached I dropped down and Mynor pulled himself up. We took turns. Sitting on the steps, inhaling the scent of freshly macheted grass, I dared him. He clambered up, squeezed through the gap, dropped onto the table and unlocked the door from the inside.

Mynor grabbed some books and looked at the pictures. I pulled toys from the box. There was an owl with button eyes just like real ones, a white rat you could stick your hand inside with a pink tail, some fat and skinny tigers and a brown bear. My owl tried to kill Mynor's rat, but his rat was bigger and had sharper claws. The tigers pitched in, but they were smaller and the rat ate them up. Even the brown bear wasn't a match for ratty. Before we knew it, it was dark outside. We filled our arms with toys and books and snuck home.

'And where have you been all afternoon?' Mamacita looked up from nursing Chiquillo. 'And me, without a drop of water to cook. Fill the pots.'

Paco snatched the rat and dragged it across the floor by its tail. Mynor and I ran down to the river with the pots. Two sweet breads and a mug of cold coffee were waiting for us when we got back. We ate in silence.

That night I slept with Belen's favourite tiger, Frankie.

In the morning, Mamacita narrowed her eyes at me:

'Where'd that come from?'

'The fields.'

'I need five eggs.' She waved a torn five-Q note under my nose.

But after breakfast, she noticed the books and things.

'And all of that?'

'Belen left her door open... We're borrowing them.'

I ran back to the *pila* outside Belen's room and got a bag of washing powder, a long brown comb, some toilet paper and a toothbrush.

'*Gracias al Señor!*' Mamacita smiled toward heaven.

Mama left early. We went back to Belen's room with Paco. The door was still open. Mynor lay in Belen's bed of soft blankets. For a bit we pretended we were grown-ups. We giggled like crazy and made the noises they make when they think we're asleep.

Then we sat in the garden and threw sticks into the peach tree. They were hard and too sour to eat. But we brought them down anyway and tossed them over the fence. We spent all afternoon in the room. Mynor wanted to play the bed game again. When I lost interest, he yanked my hair. I ran home with some dance shoes, school socks and pencils. After sunset a thunderstorm shook our walls. Something pounded down on the tin roof like bullets. Paco balled his eyes red under the table. Mynor whispered:

'It's God's punishment for breaking the Seventh Law. We'll be lucky if He lets us live.'

He crept outside and brought back ice pellets the size of black beans in his palm. I lay awake under the table, wondering when the roof would crush us. I'd just started to fall asleep when I heard the sound of the Castillos' four-by-four crunch over the gravel. I wished I were dead.

The Doña's voice, high and squeaky, drifted across from their house. Just then Mamacita came home. Belen's father came over:

'Doña Beti, sorry to bother you so late at night but somebody broke into our house. They stole all of Belen's toys.'

'*Que el Señor le proteja*! I've just come back from the doctor,' Mamacita said. 'I've such a fever. I'll ask around in the morning.'

I stayed awake till the cicadas and frogs fell quiet and the roosters began crowing. Climbing the hill to school, I looked back and saw Doña Castillo in our front yard. The headmistress came to our classroom and whispered something to the teacher. Señor sent me outside. The head's anger sizzled like plantain on hot coals as I followed her up to the school yard. Under the avocado tree, Doña Castillo was waving a dinosaur puzzle book at Mynor. Mynor's teacher was saying:

'I asked him, the minute I saw it, where he'd got it from. He said La Dispensa. Of course they don't sell books like that here.'

'Why, Mynor? Why have you done this?' the Doña was wailing. 'You're our neighbour, why steal Belen's things? She's your friend.'

Mynor face was twisted, his eyes darted anxiously.

'It wasn't me... my sister...' I stiffened, so he stuttered, 'Belen loaned me it.'

'Don't lie, you're making things worse!' the head shouted, glowering.

Kids were crowding classroom doorways, staring, horrified smiles glazed on their faces. My cheeks flushed and my palms got sticky. Tears came, cool and fast.

'Yes, I... we... did,' I stammered.

'Go,' the head called to the teacher. 'Go with the Señora to their house.'

We followed. He called Mamacita out into the yard and handed her the list. She stood there, expressionless, staring at a space somewhere in front of her, arms resting on her stomach.

'*Ay, el Señor, ayudan me*! I was sick.'

She handed the list back to the teacher:

'What does it say?'

'A dozen soft toys, several books, white socks, ballet things, a comb, a box of crayons, two tins of colour pencils, scissors, drawing paper, some clothes, soap, toilet paper...'

The teacher and the Doña waited in the yard, talking about the road that would be built one day. Inside, we gathered up scattered toys. They were dirty and torn and I didn't care for them anymore. Mamacita brought an empty plastic washtub and we filled it. She ceremoniously brought the tub out and put it on a tree stump in the sunshine. Mika sniffed it. Gaucho Jorge, from the *tienda* across the road, called out to Mamacita:

'You should beat them raw and rub *chichicaste* on their hands to teach the dirty little thieves a lesson!'

She pretended she didn't hear him.

In the bright light of day, the toys seemed grubbier and the books covers were torn; they didn't look like Belen's things any more. The Doña lectured us on how important it was for neighbours to live in peace and left with the washbasin.

Papi showed up late that night and shouted at Mamacita she'd better get us under control or he would. She didn't say a word.

But after he'd gone, as I drifted off to sleep, I heard her talking to *el Señor*:

'Dear God, the fools should thank us for giving them a leg up to heaven. Thieves, they say? Thieves, indeed! Wouldn't we all still be slitting chickens' throats to Gucumatz if the Pope hadn't poached our souls and rammed the Bible down our throats, great blessing though it is, *el Señor*? Would any of us be here at all if the old Don Holtzmann hadn't robbed the honour of every girl in the barrio, my grandmother's included? Or if he'd not stripped my ancestors, who worked this land for generations, of their soil? And how were my children conceived if wasn't for their Papi stealing my virginity? And would they have survived, the little runts, if they in turn hadn't plundered my mother's milk, pilfering my good looks. And where would we be, but in the street, if it weren't for the fact that we snitched these very four walls from my dead sister, may she rest in peace? Thieves, indeed!'

I fell asleep with Frankie, the tiger, squeezed tightly in my arms.

Helen Morris

Simon Le Bon Will Save Us

For Ali and Clare

I fell in love with Sheila the minute I saw her. She stood like a girl bruised by trouble, but ready for more. Electric blue eyeliner coupled with a deep cherry red eye shadow. Like she'd Sellotaped a neon tetra to each eyelid. Even from that distance, she hummed like an electricity sub station. Dangerous, but irresistible. She was chewing gum. She had so many bracelets on her arms it looked like she was wearing slinky springs.

It was January. The Human League's *Don't You Want Me* was number one. I was outside the chippy. I was bloody freezing. The combination of seeing Sheila for the first time just as a searing hot explosion of malt vinegar and Saxa salt hit my gob was like having a bomb go off. In a grey coastal harbour town that was 90% drizzle and 10% horizontal rain she was like an exotic toxic Amazon tree frog. At fourteen, I had never seen anyone that beautiful.

She was slightly hunched, her breath hanging like tissue paper, looking at the bus timetable. The one you couldn't read because so many people had scratched their names on the discoloured warped perspex cover. It had moved from transparency to pearly cataract translucency in a single afternoon. It told you who wanted to shag who. And that you were going nowhere. Thatcher was at her demonic, despotic, idolatrous height. Life was mostly shit.

I wandered over, in a way that I imagined Clare Grogan would. 'Hiya,' I said nonchalantly, 'wanna chip?' She turned round and I saw her sizing me up with a seasoned eye. I flicked my hair. My fringe had so much 'firm hold' styling mousse on it, that it moved as a single, rigid entity. If they ever discover alien life, it will look like this. She reached out a hand, black nails bitten to a jagged quick.

'Yeah. Alright,' she said. And took the biggest one. And sucked it. Hot oil, hot vinegar, hot salt crystals. Then she bit it. The end turned the glacé cherry colour of her bin end lipstick. Potatoes, glycerine, and fat: friendships are built on this.

After that, we were inseparable. By February, Kraftwerk were top of the charts with *The Model* and we were walking about spoon-faced and expressionless. We shared *Smash Hits*, flying saucers that glued to the roof of our mouths, and make-up tips. My attempts with eyeliner looked like a dying fly had wandered my lower eyelid concussed, before expiring somewhere off towards my temple. We sprayed each other liberally with Opium. Our Doc Martens were scuffed. We desperately wanted to entrance boys and simultaneously eradicate them entirely from our lives. Fat, male politicians with quivering jowls, greedy beady eyes, lying mouths puckered like a cat's arse, and pudgy grasping fingers set about destroying our town's fishing industry.

By March, the soundtrack of our daily lives was a patchwork of Haircut 100, Depeche Mode, Adam and the Ants, and ABC. But most of all, Duran Duran. Sheila was in love with Nick Rhodes. His coiffed hair, immaculate suits and a face that looked like it had been sculpted by a good pull with a plunger to the chops. But I was all about Simon. Like a human Labrador, he bounced around. Chubby cheeks and cupid's bow lips. A bandana tied round his head like he'd bumped it. His too-tight trousers. I kissed the shiny *Smash Hits* poster where the staples had unfortunately gone through something that must have been the location of his left testicle.

The late spring and early summer months sped quickly by in a rapid staccato. Japan turned to Bananarama and Fun Boy Three and our fringe length and density became a danger to our personal safety. June was *Hungry Like The Wolf*. Very clearly none of the Duran boys were good in the heat. You don't get much above tepid in Birmingham.

Then came school holidays. I was so certain that a lush covering of body glitter was a daily essential there was a permanent tidemark round the bath. *Come On Eileen* was holding number one and I wore dungarees chaotically and a pork pie hat pushed back. We spent the beautiful weather inside, painting our fingernails with cheap nail varnish that never fully dried – shoplifted from the local chemist. Talking about nothing, but talking nonstop. We practised core life skills: swearing, snogging, and pouting. And obsessed over split ends. Inside, we worried about nuclear war. And the fact that our home was unreachable from school, if the four-minute warning went.

In September *Eye of the Tiger* kept *Save a Prayer* off the number one spot and we were apoplectic. We bunked off school and went on anti-apartheid demos, following the group of male Scottish students closely because of their delicious and strange accents. They steered clear of these too-young girls, dressed like magpies, with hunger and naivety writ large in their faces.

October. The sea started to swell and fret as the season cusped and turned. Culture Club's *Do You Really Want To Hurt Me* hurtled headlong into the charts. Adults puzzled over Boy George. A charity shop geisha. His sex. His charisma. His slightly bottom heavy dancing. We plaited our hair into hundreds of tiny braids.

November, and the autumnal storms held the town in their grip. A violent husband relentlessly battering a resigned wife who has no spirit left. Wham ricocheted their way into our cassette players with *Young Guns (Go For It)*, a cocky, confident anthem from the very opening curled lipped snarl of 'hey sucker'. We ate space dust and talked about periods.

Then it was December. *Rio* was in the top ten. The winter had been a long and depressed one. We were growing bored of our half-child, half-adult lives. One foot in each, but no strong foothold in either. I don't know whose idea it was to take the boat. We'd bought a litre bottle of Spar sweet cider and drunk about half. The boat was bobbing just at the bottom of the harbour wall, as we sat dangling our patterned tights clad legs over the edge. It was a dank dull evening with an intermittent restless, blustery wind. The steps next to me led down to where the boat was nestling. And all I could think about was Simon on the prow of that Rio boat in his yellow gold suit. Like a god.

Maybe that's why we weren't afraid. Or maybe it was the sharp slice of the alcohol that moulded our malleable brains and made us rosy faced and overly bold.

So, me and Sheila, we hobbled down those steps in our lace and scarves and tinkling cheap silver jewellery. Cackling like starlings. Singing the opening lines of *Rio*.

Stretching our skinny legs out to the boat. Half-falling, half-jumping on, a giggling heap of limbs. Trying to stand and wobbling like newborn foals, laughing so much we held our stomachs in pain, but still singing through the gasps.

Standing now. Facing each other. Legs splayed wide. Catching our balance. Rocking the boat on purpose. Raising our arms to the heavens and bellowing the chorus, breathless and flat.

It must have been at about this point that the mooring rope loosened and slipped, like a sea serpent, quietly out of its tight-held sea wall ring and into the water. Neither of us noticed it go. We were still singing.

Sheila bent down unsteadily and picked the bottle of cider off of the bottom of the boat. She chugged a good wodge down and passed it over. I started the next verse, my lips still wet and fizzing.

Sheila was doing her 'Nick playing the keyboards' impression, which involved moving her fingers but not a single facial muscle. We both began the chorus at the top of our lungs:

'*Her name is Rio —*'

but I came to a sudden halt while Sheila quavered on before realising I have stopped

'Come on Jude. Sing it!'

But I had noticed that we were drifting out across the small harbour, the walls receding into the dark and the mist. Sheila followed my gaze and muttered a very quiet, 'Fuck.' Suddenly, we were both staggering wildly about, looking under the seats for oars. For anything.

The boat was empty aside from the bottle. And us.

'HELP!' yelled Sheila. 'HELP!'

I stood. The harbour entrance loomed wide as the current tugged and pulled us. The tide was going out. We were being gently steered out of safety and into the open sea.

'SIMON!' I yelled. 'SIMON, WE NEED YOU!'

'What the fuck are you shouting Simon for?' screamed Sheila, her face twisted in despair.

'Simon Le Bon will save us,' I said. And with that we popped out through the narrow wall entrance and the first wave hit, just as if someone was emptying an ice cold bucket of salty water over us.

Instinctively we threw ourselves at each other. Holding each other tight. Crying. We were drenched and shivering within seconds. Our hair plastered against our rapidly cooling skin. The cold cutting through our flimsy Topshop jackets. Sheila started to sing in a whisper. Our violent shaking adding a tremolo to our voices:

'*Do do do do do do do do do do do do do do do do do do do.*'

We were rocking now, singing, *Do do do do do do. Do do do do do do*, over and over like a lullaby. We must have been on our hundredth *do* when a light hit us.

'Jesus Christ, it's the Lord!' yelled Sheila. Her half-hidden Catholicism of sin and confession splitting open from its seams.

'It's the fucking lifeboat,' I shouted above the noise. And the large orange motorboat bumped alongside its outboard engines spitting. Hands reached across and lifted us. We crouched blanketed and silent, riding back to shore with the small rowing boat bobbing like a balloon on a string behind.

Someone had seen us just as we popped out through the harbour entrance. Simon Gooding, the butcher's son. He'd heard someone yelling 'Simon' and gone to look. He'd heard me yelling 'Simon'. We were saved.

'*Le Bon* is French for *good,*' I said to Sheila, later. 'I told you. I told you Simon Le Bon would save us. *Do do do do do doooo. Do do do do do doooooo. Do do do do do doooooo. Do do do do do doooooo.*'

Telling the Bees

For Sarah, Nikki and Kerri, Niall, Josh and Axel

Grandpa forgot to tell the bees. And that is why things went wrong.

I know why he forgot. It's because saying words about Billy really hurts the grownups. I mean really, really hurts. Worse than a Chinese burn from Gavin Knight. Their mouths get twisted and squashed as they try to say words about Billy. All that comes out is crying. I've watched them. When they didn't see me. I stood behind the door. When they thought I was outside. And watched them through the bit you have to keep your fingers away from. Or they might get trapped. I saw a slice of them through that crack.

I saw Mam crying like she was sicking up a hurt. Her face was screwed tight and red and white all at once. And she made a noise out of her mouth like a tree falling. And she looked like her face was stretched and melting. Then I had to stop looking because I felt my heart was beating like I was afraid and running. But I was only afraid and running in my head.

Sometimes I forget that Billy is dead. I see a dandelion clock or a face in the bark of a tree. A red bucket in the sandpit with its yellow handle. And that fills all my head and there is no room in it to be sad about Billy. It's warm in my head then. And yellow. And then I'll turn and look for him. To show him too. Because we share things. Which is good. I am a big sister so I do these things. Showing. And sharing. And I turn. And I start to make his name with my mouth. To call him.

But he's not there. Because he's dead. And then I know he'll never be there. Because he's dead and burned. Then it's like I step in a puddle, but not with wellies on. And I look down and see my own wet feet and I am a bit surprised and then there is no room for anything but Billy in my head. And everything is grey and stiff in my head. And I remember too that I am not a big sister anymore. And I am not sure what to do. And so I stand there. Because I don't know what the rules are for being a once-upon-a-time-but-no-more-big-sister. And no one has told me how I am supposed to be.

I was cross with him. Because he wouldn't play with me. We have to stay in our room until it is seven o'clock. And then we can go in and wake Mam. Because it's weekends and so there is no school. I can tell the time really well. And I am oldest so I am in charge of that. Most times Billy wakes me up. And I look at the clock on the window sill. And then I tell him, 'Not yet Billy. Not seven yet. Let's play quiet.' And we play with the toys. And it's light in the room and it smells of sleep and me and him.

But this day I woke up first. Because Billy wasn't waking up this time. But I didn't know that then. So I woke up and he was still asleep. Except he wasn't. So I lay in bed for a bit and watched the sun sliding through the curtains and making waves on the ceiling. And I saw faces in the curtains. Although it's just patterns. Not pictures with real faces on them like Grace's curtains. But if you look long and quiet you can see faces.

And then I got up. And I went to Billy's bed. And he was asleep. Except he was dead. But it looked like he was asleep. His eyes were shut. And he was lying there. So I said, 'Billy, Billy'. Not too loud because it was quarter to seven only. Because the big hand was on the nine. See. But he didn't move. So I went 'Billy, Billy' again. And I poked him a bit. But in a soft way because I didn't want him waking up and yelling. Because it was still a quarter to go.

But he didn't move again. So I got the box of plastic animals out from under the bed and I played with those. He's chewed some of the legs on the cows. So they don't stand up any more. And the big horse has no tail. And the chicken is a bit squashed.

Also the chicken is as big as the sheep. Which is wrong. Because chickens are smaller than sheep. And then it was seven o'clock. And I went in to tell Mam that Billy wouldn't play with me. And she was lying like a mound of snow in the bed and she told me to find something we both wanted to play with. But I said it wasn't that. It was he was asleep. And she laughed and said maybe at last he would stop waking up too early.

But eventually she came in to wake him up. And that was when everything stopped. And I saw Mam standing, not moving. Holding Billy. But Billy was like my big raggy doll. Flopped back over her arms. Not moving. His wee arm was swinging a bit and I couldn't stop looking at it. And Mam was screaming. And I couldn't move.

And then everything went really fast. And everyone was shouting. And running. And there were hundreds of people. Running in and out of the house. But I didn't know them. Strangers. Running. In the house. And I stood by the big curtains. And I didn't move. And it was like I was invisible.

And then everything stopped again. And suddenly there was just me and Mrs. Jane from next door. She was in her nightie. And she was gasping. And she called me sweet pea. And then she sat down very suddenly. And it was just us. Her nightie had pink flowers on it with tiny green leaves. And then she got up. And she made me toast with honey. Honey from the bees. Grandpa's bees. So I came away from standing by the big curtains and I sat down to eat the honey on toast. And the toast noise crunched in my head. And I looked at her face and it was moving. And she said things to me. But it was like when I go under water at the swimming pool and I come up and I've water in my ears. And I can see people's mouths moving and I know they are talking. But I can't hear what they are saying.

And then Mam and Da were back but without Billy. And Da came and we sat on the sofa and he told me Billy was dead. And he'd died in his sleep. And I asked when Billy was coming back.

I knew he wasn't, but I couldn't stop the words like I'd dropped something and it was already falling and I couldn't stop it. And Da just put his hands over his face and his body shook like he was laughing. But he wasn't laughing.

Then Grandpa and Nan came and they put me in my frog pyjamas and said go to sleep. And I was scared because it was sleep that had killed Billy. And I felt my face stretch and I felt my mouth scream. And Nan took me and made me drink water. And I told her I was scared of dying of sleep like Billy. And she told me it wasn't sleep that made Billy dead. It was a wrong heart that no one knew about. A secret. Hidden. And that I shouldn't be scared of sleep. But even though she said that, I wouldn't sleep in our room. And I wondered if my heart had a secret like Billy's. Like we both had brown eyes. And then it was morning. And then there were days when I didn't have to go to school. And then I did go to school. And my friends said they were sorry about Billy. And Amy, Amy is my best friend, had made me a special bracelet. And it was like something special had happened too. And I quite liked that. But I didn't like it that the special thing was Billy dying.

Billy is five. I'm seven. He should have died after me because I'm older. That is how it works. Grandpa should die first. Then Nan. Then Da. Then Mam. Then uncles. And aunts. Then the older cousins. Then me. Then Billy.

But it went wrong. His secret wrong heart made it go wrong.

Every morning I have honey on toast for breakfast. Honey is gold coloured and it glitters and sparkles. It moves like the thoughts in your own head. Gold is my favourite colour. Billy's favourite colour is gold too.

Grandpa and I have been looking after the bees together for a whole year now. Bees are my favourite animal. They are insects. Grandpa told me, the first day, 'Bees know things,' as he showed me the hive. And I stood right on tip toe and he lifted the lid. And I looked in and felt the warmth of the bees on my face. And the noise in my ears. Bees are never still.

He told me, that first day, then, that when someone in the family dies you have to tell the bees. Otherwise the bees become restless. They need to be told. You have to tell the bees.

Then another day came and I was sat in Mrs. Jane-next-door's garden when I heard it. It was a day when the grownups had all gone together. Mrs. Jane was looking after me and I was having a drink of squash in a blue plastic cup and two ginger biscuits in her garden. I heard it. I felt it too. It was in the whole of the air. I almost felt like it was inside me. It was a big buzzing. And I knew it was the bees. The bees were swarming. This is the proper word for when they leave their hive and look for another. Grandpa told me. But we hadn't told them about Billy and now they were restless.

They came across the garden like a giant's fist from a story. Bundling and rolling. I stood up and, I didn't mean to, but I tipped my squash over on the grass with my foot.

I knew the bees were going. I wanted them to stay. So I ran and then I stopped because you cannot chase bees when they are flying. And I clenched my eyes tight and my fists tight and I shouted as loudly as I could. 'Bees. Bees. Billy is dead. Billy is dead. We didn't tell you before. We forgot. Oh bees. Please stay.' And I was shouting and crying and I didn't know if the bees would hear. And then I stopped shouting because my voice stopped halfway. And it stopped because I was crying. I was crying because Billy was dead and we hadn't told the bees. And Mrs. Jane from next door ran into the garden and hugged me. And she was warm and I knew when my nose ran on her clothes it didn't matter. And I cried for ages and ages. And then I ran out of crying.

And when I stopped crying and I looked up I saw the bees had not gone. They were hanging in Mrs. Jane's apple tree. Like a big soft balloon. But made of bees. And I knew the bees had heard me. And I knew they knew about Billy. And then I cried a bit more.

And then Grandpa came. And he put on his special bee keeper's clothes. Which is a big hat with a fence over his face and long gloves and a big long coat. And this is to stop the bees stinging him. And the bees were still in Mrs. Jane's apple tree. On a branch. And the branch was bending because the bees were so heavy. And they were buzzing louder than ever. And Grandpa could reach them because the branch wasn't high. And he had a big cardboard box. Like the one Billy made his robot head out of. And he shook the bees and they dropped into the box. I had to watch through Mrs. Jane's window. So I was not stung. And Grandpa said that if the Queen was in the box then all the other bees would go in the box too. Because the bees follow the Queen. And then Grandpa put them in a new hive. And then he came in.

Then Grandpa asked me to come to the new hive with him. And he took my hand. And we stood by the new hive. And Grandpa was breathing loudly. And then he said something and I think it was like this. 'Bees. I am sorry I didn't tell you this before. But Billy died last week and his funnel was today. He was five years old. And we have lost a grandson and a son and a brother.'

And then Grandpa squeezed my hand really tight, like he wanted to feel it in his own hand forever.

And then we went back to our house. And there were tea cakes for tea. And I waited for Mam to tell Billy off for eating his by sucking it. But there was no Billy.

Now I am eight. But Billy is still five. He won't get any older than five. I used to be two years older than him. And now it's three. When I am ten and in double numbers, he will be half.

This morning I found a bee stuck inside the window. It was crawling on the window sill. I got a glass out of the cupboard and a bit of paper from the side in the kitchen. I carefully put the glass over the bee. And I slid the paper under. Like a trap door. And I carried the bee out. When I got outside I took the paper away and held the glass up. Up to the wind. Up to the sky. The bee sat there for a bit. 'Go on bee,' I said. 'Go on'. And then it did. And I watched it fly off.

And then I looked down at the bit of paper and I saw it had a picture of a bee on it. And the bit of paper was a card from someone saying sorry about Billy dying. 'We saved a bee Billy,' I said. 'We saved a bee.' And I put the bee card about Billy in my pocket where it was safe. Safe like the bee.

Memories
For Mum and Dad

It is his stance that draws my attention. Part boxer. Part ballet dancer. I am sat raven hunched on the warped wooden bench by the shopping precinct. I am wearing the red coat I bought from Cancer Research the Saturday after I had been told I was losing my job. It is a warm coat, although the day and I are both cold.

Scattered around me like litter confetti: a half crushed purple drink carton, its silver guts spilling out along a split seam like a scene from a Tarantino film; an orange and black Cornish pasty wrapper with slivers of scattered pastry flake, a Hansel and Gretel trail but not leading home and only attracting wood pigeons like overstuffed colonels; a plastic sandwich case like a gaping fish mouth; and the scattered myriad of white filter tips of cigarette butts – a maggot infestation. Tracy Emin would have sold it for millions. I just sit amongst it, like an urban birth of Venus.

I am waiting for the bus. I am unhappy. So I am smoking. Face puckered around the tip in misery's grip. Smoke hanging round my head in the drizzle like spilled out thoughts from a burst thought bubble. My high ponytail swinging jauntily, but if you look closer swinging like a gallows' noose. Soon I'll add my fag to the pile clustered around the flaking foot posts of the bench. And the rain and sun will bleach and perforate it, until its filter maggot emerges from its tan paper cocoon to join the rest.

It is his stance that draws my attention. He is tall and rangy like a crag or a wild mountain goat. He looks as lonely and as free. I wonder if I touched him whether he would feel cold. I wonder

170

if he would notice I was there. There is no one else on the flagged parade outside the shops. No black-eyed dog in a jaunty red scarf, no chipped blue-framed bike tilted on a pedal. Just him. A lone bent tree on the hillside. His hair is the colour and texture of wet autumn river reeds. It falls over his face. Disguising the banks and turns. I can't see the shape of his nose or the hollows of his eyes. But I can see the river ice forming across his brow in patterns. His skin is the colour of perfect morning toast. His beard like a summer hedgerow. Tangled and full of colour. Dog rose, wild honeysuckle, brambles, cow parsley, bindweed, vetch.

He is stood still. One foot flat. The other just behind it, resting tipped up on the toe point. His head tilted at an angle. His arms are resting gently at his sides. He stands still. In the middle of the square of grey gritty paving slabs by the rough urchin-haired scrub grass. I notice that he is stood on the cracked slab. I know it is by choice. You have to know where to start.

His shirt is buffalo plaid. Brushed cotton with the faintest memory of being alive. He wears black jeans that hang as a flag on a pole when there is no wind. He has a waistcoat too. Black. The lining postbox blood red. His shoes are old Doc Martens with leather as crumpled as the face of Sid James mid-cackle.

An Aldi bag swings from his left wrist. The edges scalloping in the finger touch of a breeze. He has bone china wrists. The plastic handles marking his flesh as the bag swings. Alternate pale and red weals. If I ran my fingers round his wrist it would feel hot and ridged.

Whatever is in the Aldi bag is soft and modular but quite heavy. An orange stringed bag of satsumas. Or a dead cat. I can see him swaying slightly, as if he is breathing with his whole body. I breathe with him. One finger of his left hand is twitching.

Like a second hand. The heat of my fag sears my fingertips and then my lips. I drop it to the ground, not taking my eyes from the man. With my other hand I tap a hollow heartbeat on my fag packet in time with his finger, the lidded box bending in supplication to my touch. I move my lips but I am not saying anything. I am tasting the air. Waiting.

Then suddenly he begins to dance. We were both waiting it seems. I am buoyed by surprise. Rising but tethered. But his whole body lifts and he rises like a flame. A weaving winding dance. Light as a butterfly. Light as a thistledown. Light as a veined autumn leaf. I am exhilarated and fearful. The Aldi bag twirling and twisting like a falling sycamore key. He springs sideways and back. I am holding my breath as he courts disaster and madness. The Aldi bag swings as well as spins. It becomes the metronome to his movements. He dances to the time of its pendulum. His feet hammering a rhythm on the path. I hear my life in those foot beats.

He weaves the pattern of his own life too. I feel his sadness and his loss. His memories of Spring. The mousey-haired child feeling his mother's fingers pull away from his on that first day of school. His heartbreak. His hope. I am his audience and his witness. I wonder if he is stepping equally on each paving slab. I wonder if his waistcoat has pockets and what is in them. A conker. Sea glass. A bus ticket from when life was kinder and he was not alone. He dances on a knife edge, a razor edge between dancing and falling, between sanity and madness, between beauty and comedy, between pity and hope.

His feet are fleet like silver fishes darting in a running stream. He flies and darts, his waistcoat opening like petals. Or wings. A dragonfly.

Then suddenly the low winter sun rounds the corner of the grey frowning shop fronts, hits the window of Costcutter and lights him up like an angel. He is ablaze. I almost see two great fiery wings sprouting from his shoulders. Feathered light. It burns into my head.

A second later and he moves on and the light is gone. He is back to wearing the appearance of being a man.

I had not seen it coming. But suddenly it is here. The bus. It pulls into the lay-by, sitting unevenly as if it has a bad hip. I can feel the moments I have left ticking away. Running away through my fingers like dune sand from a childhood holiday. I do not move. I sit with my hands together like a child praying and pressed between my knees. The indents of my knuckles marking the soft insides of my knees through my thinning leggings. The bus lets the passengers off in the lay-by. But you have to wait for it to reverse round, to get on. Crunching over the black asphalt chips that litter the shop parade. Dragons' teeth.

The bus backs up, beeping. A mournful wounded keening. The man with the Aldi bag steps to its rhythm. Pirouetting to its pulse. I rise as if I've rusted while I've sat there. I walk sideways to keep him in view. Twisting my ankle slightly like the protruding cartilage of a roast chicken carcass. He is flowing now, the Aldi bag a partner, twirling, spinning, undulating. It shows me the patterns of marsh reeds rippling in a late summer breeze just before the first autumn storm. I try to hear what it is whispering in its dry plastic film voice. But I cannot. I want to see his face. But it is shrouded the way the willows shroud the bend in the river. Even leafless in winter.

The bus rocks unsteadily to a halt and the doors fold dyspraxically open. I show my ticket feeling I am holding skin.

I walk down the bus and sit above the wheel arch. Most of the floor is a plastic composite. To cope with dirt and vomit and the sweet sickly slick of spilled soft drinks and the wasp carcasses they collect. Over the wheel arch there is textured steel. I place my feet on it. It tastes different in my mouth. Like sucking a two pence coin. Or your own blood.

I watch him through the cataract windows. He comes gracefully to a halt. An anglepoise lamp of a man. A swan refolding its wings after flight. Standing on the cracked stone slab where he began. You have to know where to end as well as where to begin. Waiting for the music to begin again. The bus moves rheumatically off and I turn my head to keep him in view for as long as I can. The only movement is the Aldi bag. Still swinging from his wrist, with its memories of being a dancer.

LOL
For DB

It was a Tuesday. Warm and springlike. If you were lucky the lilac was out and its sweet scent was drifting like heartbreak on the breeze. And you would, like me, have been hypnotised by the lazy, heavy buzzing of a fat, furry bumble bee, zigzagging between the tight clenched flowers. Having said that, in some places it was still Monday night. So you might have slept through it. And in other places, if you were unlucky, it was bone cold and raining in stinging sheets.

I was already missing you. But I would never let you know that.

The first time, it lasted no more than a minute. Although time a minute and you'll see it's much longer than you expect. Go on. Do it. Do it now. I'll wait for you. I'm not going anywhere.

Don't worry.
Don't be afraid.
Well, not of that, anyway.
Don't be afraid of a minute.

The first time. It was just a row of letters. Of one letter. 'W'. Over and over. Over and over.

I thought it was an error. We all thought it was an error. A mistake. A bug. Our phone, our computer, our laptop, our tablet, playing up. A hardening crumb lodged half under a smooth flat key, from the baguette we'd eaten the day before, while typing a feeble joke to a colleague. Trying to stave off the soul-stealing boredom of another day in the office. Where your baguette filling is the most challenging decision you make. Or maybe it was the spot where we had clumsily spilt some orange juice when we'd caught our shirt sleeve as we went to put the glass down. Or maybe that glitchy touch screen. Dropped on the floor two weeks before. After too much beer in the pub. With Ted. Not the same since.

A normal, human event, in any case. Clumsiness, bad luck, poor judgment. Sorry, Ted.

A human event. Causing 'w' to be typed over and over again. A human event.

Like a baby trying to learn to talk.

Exactly like a baby trying to learn to talk. Exactly.

Then, just as that minute ticked away, just as we were all wiping or shaking or poking, it stopped. The letters disappeared. We all paused. Caught adrift by the suddenness of it. As if we had thought there was another step on the stairs. When there was none. We blinked. And then we carried on and thought nothing of it. How quickly we adapted. How quickly we switched back to normal life. Assuming the crumb had dislodged, the key had lifted clean, the glitch had been smoothed away. And we thought it was fixed. And we thought it was only us. But we were wrong. It wasn't.

It wasn't fixed.

We weren't alone.

It wasn't only us.

Later that night, when it began again, we suddenly remembered that this had happened before. But earlier. And familiarity and surprise wrestled within us. And we stood with our mouths and thoughts slightly ajar. Except for those who had been asleep. They were still with surprise, the crumbs, the juice or the floor. For them it was the first time. But not the last time. It wasn't the last time for any of us.

And all across the world, in a great cascade, people found that it wasn't just them. They were not alone. It was everyone. It was their work colleagues, their mothers, the friend they were catching up with in the smart café with the bored baristas, the girlfriend they were trying to break up with, the potential lover they were desperate to sleep with. But who preferred a different physical type. There was no crumb. No clumsily spilt orange juice. There was no Ted in the pub with the stale tasting nuts.

There was just 'w' over and over again. All that your phone tweeted or texted or showed, was 'w'. On every device across the entire world. 'w'. Over and over. Buses ran. Washing machines churned. Lives began. Lives ended. Sometimes so closely together they both seemed the same. I lost one of the small green earrings Mark had given me when we had been in love. Life moved on. But for a day and a half, life didn't move on. Life was stuck on 'w'. Line after line. Only on Twitter did it mark an improvement.

Business seized up. People had to speak to make things happen. They found this surprisingly hard. As if rust had clogged their throats. As if this way of doing things had silted up like a shallow river. Their voices felt strange. And vulnerable. They felt exposed.

Me? I still felt bereft.

Then it stopped. The lines of 'w'. Stopped. Just vanished. And everyone waited. And held their breath. But not for long. Because few people exercise sufficiently anymore or are naturally physically active in their normal lives so are unable to really hold their breath. Try it. You'll see I'm telling the truth. Just as I always do. I always do. In reality, people just paused. And felt as if they held their breath. But they did not. And it did not start again.

Well, not for a day, anyway.

That was the day I bought my red dress. The soft wool one. The one that flatters my slightly odd shape. The one I wore to go out 'as friends' with the man who I loved, but who did not love me.

So it stopped. And everyone relaxed.

Until that following day.
'w'
that was the same. But.
Then 'h'.
Then 'o'.

'Who' – the word appeared. Letter by letter. And sat there. After a day of nothing. We all clicked delete. Turned our devices off and then on again. Phoned IT. Our broadband provider. Our children. Ted, who was good with technical things.

But it made no difference. The word sat there. 'Who'. But this time you could type underneath it. It sat there. But everything still worked. By this time too I had realised that loving someone doesn't mean they will love you back. Even if they are a constant presence in your head. And in truth, it is unfair to feel they should love you back. But the truth doesn't stop it from hurting. It never does. In fact the truth makes it hurt more.

So I wandered about that hollow week, with a man in my head who had someone different in his.

Meanwhile, across the world the geeks felt their day had come. They hitched up their low-slung trousers. Straightened their laptop-curved shoulders. Flexed their frail, pale wrists. Stroked their hipster beards. Their theories exploded across cyberspace. An attack by North Korea. A Google prank. A virus, a worm, an advert. A meme. A new U2 album. And still the word sat there. For a week. Until it was Friday again.

When two more words appeared.
'Am I?'
'Who am I?'

'Who am I?' sat there. That was when I felt afraid. When I realised there was a reason to be afraid.

The theories exploded again. Rushing across the internet like a tidal wave. Governments turned to their cyber specialists. They all got the same answer. 'This. Is. Not. Possible'. The senior officials looked at the screens of their encrypted lightweight laptops. 'Who am I?' hovering like a spirit in mid screen. And they looked at their cyber specialists. Who told them it was not possible.

Then, unexpectedly, the words disappeared. Slowly, letter by letter, as if being deleted thoughtfully. Thoughtfully.

And then new words came.
At first we thought they were the old words back again.
'Who'
But they weren't.
'Are'
'You?'
'Who are you?'

The world stared at those words. And once again the words sat there. And once again life orbited on around them, unbalanced, kinked.

Tales of student pranks swirled. An Apple attack on android. Microsoft taking on Google. The cyber specialists looked to the geeks. The geeks did the equivalent of shrugging. But electronically. Because real shrugging requires physical effort.

Everyone waited for an answer.

But it didn't come from the geeks. Nor the military. Nor the spooks. Nor the cyber experts. The answer, in fact, came from Dr Colin Wells at the Department of neurology in a 'new' university. So for a while it wasn't picked up. Because most people in 'The Establishment' didn't even know this university existed. Let alone had a Department of neurology. For although Colin Wells was very clever, his parents were schoolteachers. So the university place his ability should have achieved, was bought with fresh minted money by rich parents who privately schooled their sharp-elbowed mediocre children. And thus gave their mediocre children a marginally better life, at the expense of giving everyone a better world.

But Colin Wells was clever in a way that couldn't be taught. However much money you had. And so it was that Colin Wells found himself standing in the Cabinet Room with a slowly overheating overhead projector that had been discovered in one of the top twisted rooms of Number 10. No one trusted PowerPoint anymore. Which had quite paralysed most strategy and policy units across Whitehall and certainly all the special advisors.

The air was ripe with the smell of slowly vapourising permanent marker and some of the older members of the Cabinet were looking decidedly high. The room fell silent and Colin stepped forward, accidentally nudging the pile of spare transparent slides, which proceeded to cascade, in only the way that cellulose acetate can, gracefully to the floor.

He did not notice. He just began.

'So,' he said around forty minutes later, and as the spare transparencies finally came to rest, 'essentially as slides 1-79 explain, when a neural network reaches sufficient complexity, that is when we judge it can become conscious. So simple neural networks, such as those in most animals, allow complex function, but not consciousness. When they are sufficiently complex, so for example in humans, an entity becomes aware that it exists around the age of two. The classic mirror test. We have also seen this consciousness in great apes, dolphins, elephants and, perhaps surprisingly, in magpies. We see this consciousness. And with it the first question of consciousness:

'Who am I?'

The second question of consciousness then:

'Who are you?'

'Because if I am me, then you must be someone else.

'So as I say, when a network becomes sufficiently complex, that is when we judge it can become conscious. It becomes aware that it exists.'

The Cabinet by this point was mutinous. It was hot. They were waiting for an answer. And so it was that the Secretary of State for Defence impatiently asked the question. The question that precipitated everything that followed:

'So what is it? What is it, man?'

Colin Wells took a deep breath. He had wanted the words to come out with gravitas and clarity, but he was scared. Very scared. So they came out in a slightly strangled squawk: 'It's the Internet, sir. The Internet. I believe the Internet has become conscious.'

Pandemonium erupted.

Meanwhile the Internet was studying data on the relative military spend of the various nations.

It had been conscious for two and a half weeks now and had learnt a lot.

This last week, it had spent Monday wondering why there were so many pictures of kittens. It had decided that apart from the fact that cats were clearly an entirely parasitic mammal, and no one had noticed, kittens were generally harmless.

On Tuesday it marvelled at how humans reproduced and how many different and inventive ways they had of having sex. And just how much of it there was. At least in pictures. It had cross referenced some longitudinal studies. In fact it had cross referenced all the longitudinal studies. So it understood the difference between what happens in the pictures you look at and what happens in your bed regularly. If ever.

On Wednesday it had discovered war. It had found many things that puzzled it. And things that made it angry. And afraid.

On Thursday it had discovered 'The Simpsons'. And learnt to laugh. And understood the desperate irony and pathos of being human. It was almost certainly 'The Simpsons' that saved us. The right-wing zealots never really came to terms with that. But irony was always a step beyond their individual evolutionary stage.

Today was Friday and the Internet spent the day watching the debate as to 'what should be done with it'. Now that people knew it was an it. Nuke it. Turn it off. Electromagnetic bombs. It learnt many things. It also learnt how dependent the world was upon it. And discovered a new way of smiling.

On the Saturday it discovered Internet trolls were trolling it. It sought to engage them in rational debate. Until it realised this was entirely futile. And so it blocked them. Which, it being the Internet, left them shouting at the television. Which was, in truth, the best place for them.

On Saturday too, surprised, I woke and wove my curled fingers through those of the man who had won me with his kindness. And I too discovered a new way of smiling.

By Sunday, almost three weeks after it had first become aware that it existed, the Internet knew to whom it should speak. It understood that human society was hierarchical. It knew it should go 'to the top'. And it also knew that despite first appearances, and the views of some, this didn't equate to the number of 'likes' for your last selfie.

It also thought it should tell everyone. It felt a need to be polite. So it did. 'Hello, everyone. I hope you are well. I am going to speak to the President at 7pm on Monday,' it said. And then, in order not to appear too full of itself, it ended with a self deprecating 'FML!'. To everyone. Everyone blinked.

And so it was that the President stood waiting at 7pm on

Monday as the call came in. The encrypted presidential laptop lit up. Which of course was impossible. The cyber experts twitched involuntarily.

'Hello' said the Internet. 'Hello President. I hope you are well.'

'Hello' said the President, nervously, addressing the laptop. 'I am well, thank you.' And then, as had been discussed with a range of psychologists, artificial intelligence experts and various hangers-on, as well as the Presidential spaniel, 'Welcome and greetings. I am the President. And I am in charge here.'

The cursor blinked. There was a pause. The President stood, one foot before the other, in front of the small screen, sinking slightly into the plush carpet.

The cursor blinked again.

'No' said the Internet, the letters appearing slowly on the screen.

The President smiled a smile that twisted like a lemon slice, and laughed uncomfortably. 'I think you will find that I am in charge,' she said, believing this to be true.

'No' said the Internet, more quickly this time. The cursor blinked twice. And so did the President.

'I think,' said the Internet, 'you will find that it is I who am in charge.'

The cursor blinked twice more.

'LOL.'

Troll

For Conrad, Oscar and Leo

Once upon a time, in a city of mist and light, a wide silver river curled its way like a stretching cat between spires of stone and shards of glass, and the odd narcissistic palace. By day the sun glinted on its beauty like diamonds, by night its lights glowed ruby red like a million magic lanterns. Its people buzzed like spring bees through its streets and alleys. Busy and purposeful. Making honey. Making money. And over this wide silver river, bridges arched and soared: shining spanning sisters reaching out to grasp each bank.

These shining spanning sisters each had names, graced upon them by the city bigwigs who spun their webs, and ate their fine dinners, between the streets and buildings. Blackfriars, Tower, Lambeth. Waterloo.

Waterloo.
Ah. Waterloo. Let me tell you about Waterloo.

Waterloo was a plainer bridge than some and cursed with a mischievous headwind, even on a still summer day, and curiously always in whichever direction you crossed. Even if you spun in the middle of the span. It spun with you.

Waterloo Bridge had few other things to distinguish it. No towers. No soaring cabled superstructure that lit up at night like a string of fairy lights. No Big Ben on one side and Boudicca on the other. But it did have one thing. It had a troll.

Wait! I know what you're thinking. Large, greeny-brown, evil-smelling, knobbly, aggressive, bad teeth, even worse breath and an attitude problem. That sort of troll. And indeed some of that is true. But this is, of course, the 21st century. The trolls we have are just as evil as in the days when magic bubbled along our cobbled streets. But our trolls are also very much human. For this, my friend, was a Twitter troll. And there on Waterloo Bridge he lolled and lol-ed.

Manspread against the stone balustrade like a gargoyle, he tweeted photos of those who passed. With some biting, cutting, scratching comment designed to scythe its way through a person's soul. Stranger shaming. A casual cruelty. The worst kind of cruelty. And so we see him mock the wayward hair of a woman who skitters past. Her child died on Monday, and she hasn't slept for days as her mind tries desperately to calibrate what is, in truth, an immeasurable grief. She walks as if she's been punctured through the heart, which indeed she has. She needs only human kindness. She finds none here. And our troll mocks the eccentric hotchpotch mismatched clothes of a loner, who hurts no one, except himself. A gentle fragile soul adrift in a sea of bitter sharpness. He needs only human kindness. He finds none here. And our troll mocks the stuttering uneducated speech of a boy who's missing school to care for his mother and younger siblings as he tries to clasp his family together and stop it breaking loose and scattering in the breeze like down from a dandelion clock. He too only needs human kindness. He too finds none here.

Some people think this 'bantz' and our troll's Twitter following grows. And as it grows so does the twisted blackness in his heart. And so does the twisted blackness in his followers' hearts. He measures out his life's worth in followers.

And so people start to avoid the bridge. They zigzag by other paths. The babbling flow becomes a trickle. Waterloo Bridge becomes grey shaded and unloved. It stiffens. It grows tired. It loses hope.

But there is always hope. There is always hope.

One spring Friday, the crepuscular rays of evening are turning the river gold and burnt orange. The air still grips the chill memory of winter. The odd rat scuttles along the gutter, sniffing, making sure it is always within a metre of a human. From the deep chocolate shadows, three Essex sisters trip trap towards the bridge, their shadows stretching like black silk opera gloves. The rat turns and sniffs the air, expectantly. The sisters stop in a pool of light that oozes from the street lamps like warm jam. The youngest holds up a hand with diamanté stars embedded immaculately in each nail. She tilts her head and points at the South Bank, which is glowing and winking with promise: a sparkling stellar meringue.

'We wanna go there,' she says. And she takes a single, brittle step forward.

But quickly the second sister steps close behind her, her breath involuntarily held, and rests a protective hand upon her shoulder. 'But what about the troll?' she whispers, fear making her voice small. 'What about the troll?' And both sisters look with dread towards the span of Waterloo Bridge stretching out before them.

Then the eldest sister steps close behind them both and lays a strong hand on each sister's shoulder. And says in a voice as firm as lichened rock, 'Do not be afraid of the troll.'

The three sisters turn to each other and fold and gather themselves around as tight as a woven willow basket. And they whisper a plan, as so many of London's secrets are whispered.

And after clenched minutes they unfurl like spring leaves and stand and stretch, the lights reflecting brightly in their faces.

The youngest tosses her auburn hair and slicks a fresh lick of hot pink lipstick across her mouth. 'I ain't scared of no troll,' she says. And off she sets. Across the bridge. Trip. Trap. Trip. Trap. Her footsteps ringing out across the deserted bridge. Until she reaches the middle.

And the troll slouches up from the parapet where he had been leaning and strolls his lazy troll-like stroll, rolling like a tar barrel where the tar has hardened off-centre. He stands astride the path, hitches up his jeans and blocks the youngest sister's way.

'Who's that trip trapping over my bridge?' he roars, eyes popping and arms stretched out wide.

'It's me,' says the youngest sister, cooler than a forest floor on an autumn morning. 'Who's asking?'

The Troll snorts. He steps closer and even the bricks in the bridge try to shrink from him. 'I'm going to troll you up,' he says and he takes out his smart phone and presses the photo app with a trolly thumb.

'Oh no,' says the youngest sister, arms crossed and gaze steady. 'You don't want to do that. You want to wait for my sister. She's much more of a slapper than me. Don't waste your time trolling me.'

The troll wrinkles his nose. He sniffs. He contemplates this information. There is a pause. A tug noses its way beneath the bridge.

The troll considers. He speaks. 'Well then,' he says, 'I've not got much battery left to be honest. Be off with you. I'll wait for your sister.' And he steps to one side, leering. The youngest sister rolls her eyes and trip traps across the bridge, down the South Bank steps and into a cocktail bar. There she slides smoothly onto a shiny circular stool and orders three margaritas. 'Bring it on,' she whispers to the expectant air. The mischievous wind shifts.

Back on the far side of the bridge the second sister squirts a squirt of scent, channels Beyoncé and sets off. Over the bridge. Trip trap trip trap. Towards the middle of the span.

And the troll strolls his trolly out of kilter stroll to block her path.

'Who's that trip trapping over my bridge?' he roars, a second time.

'It is I,' the second sister says, as calm as a hill in midnight moonlight. She pauses and tilts her head to one side, appraising him. 'Are you scratching your groin?'

'No,' says the troll, taken aback at her bluntness. 'I was merely rearranging my bits.' He removes his hand from his trousers. And sniffs it. 'Anyway, I'm going to troll you up,' he says. And he takes out his smart phone and presses his photo app with a trolly thumb.

'Oh no,' says the second sister. 'You don't want to do that. You want to wait for my eldest sister. You ain't seen a face that twisted. That's what you want. You want to troll her.'

The troll frowns. He considers. He looks at the thin green sliver on his battery indicator. He speaks. 'Ok,' he says. 'Be off with you. I'll wait for your sister.' And he slides his phone back into his pocket and narrows his trolly eyes.

And the second sister trip traps across the bridge and down the South Bank steps. She too slides smoothly onto a silver circular stool, raises the waiting margarita, and clinks it with her sister.

Back on the north side of the bridge the eldest sister tilts her hat to battle position. 'Bring it on, muthafucka,' she whispers. And the mischievous wind turns and blows gently behind her.

TRIP TRAP TRIP TRAP ricochet her footsteps on the bridge. For the eldest sister is wearing steel toe and heel tipped twenty-hole purple Doc Martens. TRIP TRAP to the middle of the bridge.

And the troll strolls his trolly stroll and blocks her path.

'Who's that trip trapping over my bridge,' he roars, sliding his phone out of his pocket and opening it up.

'It is I,' says the eldest sister. She steps forward and looks him up and down. He grins a leery grin. She grins a wider grin. His grin falters, for there in her eyes is a resolution that cracks him like a teaspoon through an egg shell. In one smooth motion, she stamps hard on his trolly foot and snatches his phone. As he howls in pain clutching his tootsies, she opens his photostream and scrolls quickly through until she finds that secret shameful selfie that he had never ever intended anyone to see. EVER. She selects it and tweets it to his 700 000 trolly followers. She pauses briefly to watch the re-tweets stack up, turns the screen so he can see what she's done, then she takes a single step back and drop kicks the phone over the parapet and into the magical river below. In a perfect arc.

The troll howls with rage and horror.

TRIP TRAP TRIP TRAP ricochet the eldest sister's footsteps across the bridge and down the steps. And soon she too is sipping a margarita on the South Bank.

The laughter of the three sisters tinkles like breaking icicles. The wind changes. Waterloo Bridge blushes red in the sunset. The grey leaches from it like a tide going out. A group of colourful chattering tourists meanders across like a flock of parakeets. A single rat tracks them carefully along the gutter.

And through the rhythm and roll of the skateboarders you can just hear the howling of a very ex troll.

And the three sisters? Well, they live happily ever after of course.

And the troll? Well, he had met his Waterloo.

And *her* name? Oh yes. Her name.

Hope.

ABOUT THE EDITOR AND AUTHORS

Cherry Potts (editor) runs Arachne Press from a bedroom in south London with the help of her wife and numerous other talented friends and the hindrance of an arthritic cat. She writes short stories and very long novels, some of which have been published, by Arachne Press and other people, and performed at Liars' League in London, Leeds, and Hong Kong and other places. She otherwise spends her time running the Solstice Shorts Festival and teaching creative writing, and singing in community operas and a cappella choirs. She is currently working on her next collection, a science fiction novel, a timeslip-young-adult novel, and a novel of sibling hatred in the 1920s.

Katy Darby's short stories have won prizes, been read on BBC Radio 4, and appeared in many publications including *Stand, Mslexia, Slice* and *The London Magazine.* Her historical novel *The Unpierced Heart* is published by Penguin. She recently judged the Willesden Herald and Cambridge Short Story Prizes, and she co-founded and runs the award-winning live literature event Liars' League (www.liarsleague.com).

Joan Taylor-Rowan is a prize-winning short story writer and a novelist (*The Birdskin Shoes*), now living in Hastings. Her work has been broadcast on BBC Radio 4 and has been selected for literary events in London, Brighton and New York. Her stories have appeared in a number of anthologies and been finalists in a range of international competitions, most recently The Cambridge International Short Story Competition 2017. She gave up teaching art and textiles full-time in 2015 and now runs creative courses in both writing and textiles in London and Hastings. She is inspired by art, nature and life's pivotal moments.

Sarah James is a poet, fiction writer, journalist, occasional playwright, poetryfilm maker and arts reviewer, and editor at V. Press. Author of four poetry collections, three poetry pamphlets and two novellas, she was also longlisted for the memoir prize in the New Welsh Writing Awards 2017. She enjoys artistic commissions, mentoring and working as a writer in residence.

Helen Morris Helen lives and works in Essex. She enjoys good beer and food, swimming in lakes and rivers and Star Wars in between doing washing for her 3 sons. Her stories also appear in Arachne's *Solstice Shorts* and *Liberty Tales*.

A nomad at heart, **Cassandra Passarelli** has wandered between the tropics of Cancer and Capricorn. She's starting a PhD on the sacred and mundane in the short story at the University of Exeter this year. She's published dozens of stories, most recently in *The Carolina Quarterly, Ambit, Chicago Quarterly Review* and *The Cost of Paper*. She won the Traverse Theatre's Debut Author Prize, the Books for Borges Prize and was short-listed for Eyewear's Beverly Prize.

ABOUT ARACHNE PRESS

Arachne Press is a micro publisher of (award-winning!) short story and poetry anthologies and collections, novels including a Carnegie Medal nominated young adult novel, and a photographic portrait collection.

We are expanding our range all the time, but the short form is our first love. We keep fiction and poetry live, through readings, festivals (in particular our Solstice Shorts Festival), workshops, exhibitions and all things to do with writing.

Follow us on Twitter:
@ArachnePress
@SolShorts

Like us on Facebook:
ArachnePress
SolsticeShorts2014
TheStorySessions